P9-DJA-901

Praise for _Seduction in Mind_

"Johnson delivers another fast, titillating read that overflows with sex scenes and rapid-fire dialogue."
—_Publishers Weekly_

"It's a spellbinding read and a lot of fun. . . . Johnson takes sensuality to the edge, writing smoldering stories with characters the reader won't want to leave."
—_The Oakland Press_

**And praise for
SUSAN JOHNSON**

"Her romances have strong, intelligent heroines, hard, iron-willed men, plenty of sexual tension and sensuality and lots of historical accuracy. Anyone who can put all that in a book is one of the best." —_Romantic Times_

"No one . . . can write such rousing love stories while bringing in so much accurate historical detail. Of course, no one can write such rousing love stories, period."
—_Rendezvous_

"Susan Johnson writes an extremely gripping story. . . . With her knowledge of the period and her exquisite sensual scenes, she is an exceptional writer."
—_Affaire de Coeur_

"Susan Johnson's descriptive talents are legendary and well-deserved." —_Heartland Critiques_

"Fascinating . . . The author's style is a pleasure to read."
—_Los Angeles Herald Examiner_

SUSAN JOHNSON

BLONDE HEAT

BANTAM BOOKS

BLONDE HEAT

A Bantam Book/June 2002

All rights reserved.

ISBN 0-553-58255-0

Published simultaneously in the United States and Canada

Bantam Books are published by Bantam Books, a division of
Random House, Inc. Its trademark, consisting of the words "Bantam
Books" and the portrayal of a rooster, is Registered in U.S. Patent and
Trademark Office and in other countries. Marca Registrada. Bantam
Books, 1540 Broadway, New York, New York 10036.

PRINTED IN THE UNITED STATES OF AMERICA

OPM 10 9 8 7 6 5 4 3 2 1

BLONDE
HEAT

It occurred to Lily, as she stood on her cabin deck gazing out on Burntside Lake, that she should have known she'd made a mistake the time she'd brought Brock here. He'd looked out at the sparkling water and majestic pines, the perfect blue sky dotted with perfect fluffy white clouds, ignored the eagle with the eight-foot wingspan soaring overhead, swatted the mosquito on his arm, and said, irritably, "I hope that doesn't stain linen. As if there'd be a decent dry cleaner in this godforsaken wilderness anyway." He'd gone inside muttering and hadn't come out again until it was time to leave two days later.

One damned mosquito.

She should have gone with her gut feeling then.

It would have saved her a helluva lot of trouble. Not to mention a divorce.

But, hey, she was here now and he wasn't and that was good. More than good. Now if she could only figure out how to turn on the water, she could wash her hands after hours on the road from Chicago and life would be great.

The phone rang, the world intruded on her mini therapy session, and she walked back inside.

"Welcome home, Juju."

Lily leaned against the kitchen counter and smiled at the greeting from long ago. "How did you know I was here? I just walked in the door."

"Myrtle Carlson saw you pull into your driveway and called her sister Olga who called my aunt Bernie who called me. And I would have phoned sooner but my aunt had to tell me about her tomato plants and the last Eastern Star meeting that almost ended in fisticuffs when Addie Montgomery and Blanche Kovar both wanted to be president. When are you coming over?"

"After I figure out how to turn on the water."

"Hurry, because Serena's on her way now. Call Bianchich's. They'll send someone over."

"Serena's home too?"

"Reluctantly. You know how she hates this town. But her mom broke her hip and needed someone to run the store for a few months. We'll fill you in when you get here. Dumped the Brock, I hear. About time."

"What happened to 'I'm sorry your marriage didn't work out. You must be distraught.'"

"I met the Brock, hon. I repeat, about time."

Lily sighed. "How did everyone know but me?"

"You're way too sweet, Juju. That's always been your problem. You believe what people say. But hey, Serena and I will show you the true path. She's in purdah here till fall and I'm at the lake all summer as usual. Now call Bianchich's about your water. If you're lucky our local hero will make the house call himself. Darling Billy still works in the hardware store every off season."

"I wouldn't recognize him if I saw him. He's years younger."

"He's also, I think the term is, good enough to eat. And if you came to your cabin more often, you'd know it."

Lily laughed. "Your libido is cranked up notches higher than mine. And I'm only just divorced. Don't talk to me about men right now."

"You know what they say about falling off that horse . . ."

"Give me a break. Unlike you, I've actually gone more than a week without sex."

"Bite your tongue. I'm on day six. Now, call the hardware store. We'll see you in an hour."

The phone went dead. Ceci had never been good about waiting for anything—which accounted for her very active sex life.

Lily didn't hear the truck pull up; she was unpacking in the bedroom. And if there had been a knock on the door, she'd missed that too. What she didn't miss were the very broad shoulders on the tall man with spiky black hair who was filling the doorway into her utility room when she went in search of more hangers.

She actually squealed when she saw him, which was embarrassing enough in itself, but when he turned around, he had such a look of amazement she realized he wasn't used to frightening people. And a second after that, she also realized Ceci was right. If this was darling Billy, he *did* look good enough to eat.

"Sorry. I didn't know anyone was at home. The work order just said the water was out." Lily Kallio's tanned legs went clear to the ceiling as they always had . . . well, almost; they stopped at— Billy jerked his glance away. "This shouldn't take long," he muttered, turning away, overcome by a schoolboy nervousness. Jesus, he felt as if he were fourteen all over again—he used to watch her sitting on the lifeguard tower at Shagawa Beach, tanned and beautiful in her pure white suit with the tiny Red Cross symbol about three inches from her crotch, wondering if she'd give him mouth to mouth if he pretended to drown, wondering if anyone would notice if he jacked off behind the dressing rooms. He never did either, although she was his nighttime fantasy for all of ninth grade until she graduated from high school and left town.

My God, the man was enormous. So much bigger than Brock, Lily thought, as though it mattered. And much more handsome, some perverse inner voice insisted on pointing out. Capable of home repairs too. Have you thought of that? And his very large hands . . .

It took her a moment to come to her senses, to stop *looking*, and a second more to tamp down the curious heated flutter warming her senses, and a second after that to say in a cool, polite voice, "Thanks for coming," and escape into her bedroom.

The word *come* struck the NHL's best winger and MVP three years running with a particular intensity. His body's involuntary reflex brought him to a momentary standstill and thirteen years flashed by in a time-warp moment. Swearing softly, he shook his head in an attempt to clear his mind of boyish fantasies. And then he said, "Fuck and double fuck," in an explosive breath and surveyed the array of copper pipes, looking for the turn-off valve.

Lily didn't come out of the bedroom until she heard the kitchen door slam and the sound of the truck driving away, even though she told herself she was acting like a child, even though she told herself it was perfectly all right if some guy turned her on like a damned spigot with one glance at his handsome face and perfect body.

Watching from the kitchen window as the Ace Hardware truck disappeared down the sandy drive, Lily was still shocked at her physical reaction to the man. She wasn't impulsive by nature—she'd earned her Ph.D. in five years because she wasn't; she was focused and deliberate. Her TV spots on the six and ten o'clock news had risen to first place in the Chicago TV ratings because she was absolutely single-minded in her goals. Even her decision to divorce had required a spreadsheet analysis . . . although in all honesty she was really fast on the computer; she couldn't kid herself any due deliberation had come into that decision once she'd seen Brock's e-mail correspondence with his lover. But with the exception of her rather precipitous divorce, she was really the least likely person to get carried away.

But darling Billy's muscles were practically bulging through his T-shirt, weren't they, and his sheer *size* sent a little shiver up her spine, not to mention his very, very large hands that made her speculate quite unintentionally on the old saw about the correlation between . . . ohmygod.

Maybe it *had* been too long since she'd had sex.

CHAPTER **2**

"It's been *way* too long since you've had sex," Ceci said an hour later, after all the down-and-dirty details of Brock's affair with his coanchor, Lily's divorce, and her upcoming year-long sabbatical in Ely had been thoroughly dissected. After they had commiserated with Lily and agreed that Brock was a shit.

Serena rolled her eyes. "Two whole months. I'd die. Don't you miss a man *doing* things for you?"

Ceci smiled. "Or share in the doing—there's a concept." Ceci's notion of good sex was a mutual give-and-take as long as the man could keep up with her; her ownership of the phrase *female assertiveness* was legend.

"I don't like to get sweaty," Serena said with the sublime insensitivity that somehow didn't seem to matter to the men who pursued her. Ceci and Serena could hardly be more different in their approach to human sexual affairs.

Lily gazed at her friends over the rim of her glass. "Until I saw the repairman from Ace Hardware, I hadn't been inclined to get sweaty of late either. Or maybe that kind of sweaty, ever." Her nostrils flared faintly. "I don't know if it's him or me, whether abstinence is affecting my thinking or he's just unbelievably hot."

"Billy's hot," Ceci said, kissing her fingertips.

"Darling Billy," Lily murmured, her earlier description of him having elicited a "Bingo" from Ceci. "He has the absolutely widest shoulders and—"

"Sweetest ass. Don't tell me you didn't notice."

"Maybe in passing," Lily said with a studied nonchalance, although the label on the back of his jeans, along with everything else underneath the label, was crystal clear in her brain.

The women were sitting on Ceci's porch six cabins down from Lily's, drinking Aunt Bernie's frozen margaritas—in good supply in Ceci's freezer along with Bernie's spaghetti sauce made from her famous homegrown tomatoes. The afternoon was sunny and warm, the breeze off the lake sufficient to keep the mosquitoes at bay, and except for Lily's lack of sex—now that she'd had the good sense to get rid of Brock—all was right with the world.

Well, sort of.

Serena had already expressed her disgust with

having to actually appear at the store each day. As a trust-fund baby, she had no aptitude for work. She didn't take after her mother, who thrived on her mission to offer artisans' wares to the world, nor had she one iota of her banker father's work ethic. Luckily, the store manager, Emily Riggs, was more than competent.

Ceci had walked out on her latest boyfriend a week ago because the sex was getting boring—a not uncommon complaint for her. "Oliver actually said, 'Was it good for you?' " Ceci had said with disgust. "If they have to ask, it usually isn't and it wasn't." Directing one of her brook-no-interference glances at Lily, she now said, "*You* need some sex, and I need some damned variety."

"I'm only going to sleep with men under twenty-five this summer," Serena declared, a completely-out-of-character defiance in her tone.

Ceci's brows flickered. "Because Homer went back to his wife. So, fuck him. No offense, darling, but why do you waste your time on rich old men anyway?"

Serena's brows dipped toward her perfect nose as she considered her answer. "They're comfortable . . . and of course—rich. Don't look at me like that. I like men to buy nice things for me. I'm sorry." Her gaze brightened. "Did I show you what Homer brought me from Paris?" She held out her slender hand.

"Nice. You could light the football field with that diamond. It works out, then," Ceci said, kindly. "Good jewelry in place of hot sex."

Serena surveyed her friend with a lazy glance. "I like sex, just not constantly like you."

"And for sure, no head-banging sex." Ceci's brows rose. "I don't know if you're going to like that young stuff."

"Maybe I'll just read this summer," Serena pronounced.

"And maybe I'll become a nun."

"And maybe I'll see if Billy Bianchich is really as big as he looks," Lily said.

"Way to go." Ceci held up her thumb. "It must be the two margaritas."

"Three. And he's really fine. Did I mention how much bigger he is than Brock?"

"Not more than ten times." Ceci offered Lily a benevolent smile. "You know what they say about hockey players . . ."

Serena looked thoughtful. "I'm not sure we have hockey players in Miami."

"You do. The Florida Panthers. They're an expansion team that's doing quite well, or at least they were until their—"

"So what about hockey players?" Serena interrupted, uninterested in sports.

"Lily knows," Ceci said, looking entertained. "She's blushing."

"Am not. It's hot in the sun."

Serena looked from one to the other. "Obviously, this has something to do with sex."

Ceci shrugged. "Hockey players have groin muscles so conditioned by the sport, they can last all night. That's all."

"All night?" Serena looked stunned.

"Only Venezuelan chocolate rivals an all-nighter for first place on my top ten list," Ceci noted. "Depending on my current obsession, of course. And speaking of obsessions"—she surveyed her friends—"I suggest we go to happy hour at the Birch Lake Saloon and check out the merchandise."

"Do you think he'll be there?" Between the liquor and all the allusions to groin muscles, Lily was getting pretty focused.

"If he isn't, I'll find him for you. This is a small town and you haven't had sex for two months." Ceci grinned. "Consider it my mission from God."

"Homer can go to bloody hell," Serena said, suddenly gripped by a missionary spirit of her own. "So can his wife and children and dog, along with his yacht and villa in Tuscany and his apartment in Manhattan where he tries to hide his family pictures before I come."

"Apparently without success," Ceci observed dryly. "Hey, I think we're on a roll here—what better time to take a fresh look at the path to nirvana? Fuck all our old boyfriends, figuratively speaking, of course"—she glanced at Lily—"and fuck no-good ex-husbands—"

"And their stupid and/or sly coanchors who 'accidentally' send their e-mail love notes to me." Lily lifted her glass. "I'll drink to that."

Ceci made the universal Italian gesture of contempt. "Fuck. Them. All."

Serena raised her glass, her short platinum curls a halo of sunlight. "Today," she began, a note of drama in her voice, "on Burntside Lake, at"—she glanced at her Bulgari diamond-studded watch—"six-thirty central daylight time—" She giggled. "I think I'm getting drunk."

Ceci tapped her wristwatch. "Five-thirty and you are."

"Sshh . . ." Serena waved her glass, dripping margaritas on the porch. "I'm not finished. Today we pledge ourselves to personal fulfillment, good friendship"—she smiled affectionately at both women—"strong groin muscles, men under twenty-five, and"—she took a small breath—"the ultimate Zen-perfect, lovely orgasm."

"Or a Catholic-perfect, lovely orgasm. Those I know—starting with Jimmy Lorenzo in Sister Theresa's cloakroom." Ceci stretched like a lazy cat. "I still think of him with fondness . . ."

"Right now, I'll settle for any kind of orgasm." Lily emptied her glass. "And it's not the liquor talking." She stood up with a grin. "It's the liquor screaming. Who's driving?"

CHAPTER 3

"Y ou're panting, Bianchich. It's not a pretty sight."

"Lay off, Zuber."

St. Louis County's only sheriff who could call the governor "Cousin Jesse" raised his eyebrows and grinned. "He's in luuuvvv . . ."

"You'd be too, if you'd seen her." Immune to the teasing, Billy sprawled in the corner of a Birch Lake Saloon knotty-pine booth etched with generations of initials and smiled. "You still salivate when you see Shelly Castelano even if she's married, with three kids."

Nick Zuber grimaced. "So I didn't want to get married at nineteen."

"I didn't say you should have." If Zuber married at forty, Billy would be surprised. As the most sought-after guide in the boundary waters, not to mention the record holder for snowmobile racing, the canoe sprint across Shagawa Lake, and the largest muskie caught in North America, Zuber's life was focused on the physical. That went for women too. With the growing fame of the boundary waters, his legion of female fans had reached countrywide proportions.

"Speaking of fantasies," Frankie Aronson said. "I saw Serena Howard at her mom's store."

Billy grinned. "That leaves Ceci for you, Zuber. Think you can handle her?"

"It wasn't a problem last time."

"Last time?" his friends said in unison.

Zuber tipped back in his chair, the cleated rubber soles of his hiking boots balanced on the edge of the booth seat. "She spends every summer at the lake."

"And?" Frankie said.

He looked at them from under his lashes. "She's worth keeping to myself."

Billy grinned. "That's why you took a sudden interest in poetry a couple of summers ago." Ceci had had some of her poetry published in *The New Yorker*.

Zuber returned his smile. "Poetry's not so bad."

"I'll bet. Rewarding even."

"Definitely rewarding."

"The three blondes," Frankie murmured, as you'd say, This Ferrari is mine, his voice husky and low and happy. "It's been a long time since they were in town together."

"Since forever. Jesus . . . fucking . . . Christ." Zuber smiled slowly, his gaze on the front door.

Everyone else in the bar was looking as well at the three women standing on the threshold. Lily was the tallest, all cool, Nordic beauty, looking like a Ralph Lauren model ready for a bike ride or a hike in her white linen blouse and khaki shorts, her honey-blonde hair gleaming. Serena's platinum curls were cropped almost mannishly short, but she'd never be mistaken for a man in her purple Capris and well-filled chartreuse halter top. Ceci's tawny hair was swept back behind her ears, her body was all bodacious curves, and she was showing it off in hip-hugging jeans and a red Dolce & Gabbana top that looked as if it had been made from a very small handkerchief.

Billy was on his feet first, but then he was known for his speed on the ice. He was halfway across the room before most people had released their breath. "I didn't introduce myself this afternoon," he said a second later, smiling at Lily. "Billy Bianchich." He gestured in the direction of his friends. "Would you care to join us?"

"Do fish swim?" Ceci wasn't shy.

"Good. Perfect." But Billy shot a glance at Lily, just to make sure.

"I'd love to," she said, thinking she was ridiculously, outrageously happy just standing next to him—almost giddy. Could Bernie have drugged the margaritas?

As Billy led them to the booth, Ceci slipped her arm through Lily's. "He *does* look big," Ceci whispered. "I want to know just how big"—she was smiling a Cheshire-cat smile—"in the morning."

Introductions were made and everything fell into place, smoothly, effortlessly, like the well-rehearsed steps of Ginger Rogers and Fred Astaire. Lily and Ceci slipped into the booth opposite each other. Serena sat in the chair Frankie pulled up for her. Zuber slid in next to Ceci, putting his arm around her shoulders and leaning close to whisper in her ear.

Serena and Lily looked at them, then at each other.

"You've met before," Serena said.

Ceci leaned into Zuber's chest, which was clothed in a T-shirt reading "Fish Fear Me, Women Love Me," and smiled. "I'm home every summer."

"Tell me more."

Ceci's gaze narrowed. "And you're not home every summer."

Serena wasn't easily rebuffed. "You're holding out, darling . . . so what's with this relationship?"

"End of discussion, Serena," Ceci said softly, the threat in her tone blatant enough even for Serena.

"Were we having a discussion?" Zuber asked, alarmed at the word *relationship*.

Ceci shook her head. "Nothing to discuss."

He looked relieved.

"Drinks?" Frankie offered, his diplomacy honed by refereeing domestic skirmishes that got enough out of hand to call the cops. He waved over a waitress and before long it felt like old home week. They talked about the summers at the lake, of high school and the teachers they'd shared, of skiing at Black Ridge, and of keg parties out in the woods.

Everyone exchanged truncated versions of their life since Ely High School, brief descriptions of college, careers, family. And then, intent on her mission, Ceci said, "Lily just cut loose the world's worst husband. She needs cheering up."

Lily turned cherry-red even under the neon bar signs. "Jeez, Ceci, if you don't mind . . ."

"That calls for a pitcher of Molly Bee's special cheer-up potion," Zuber declared. "Pink or green?"

While Lily and Serena looked puzzled, Ceci said, "Pink with extra cherries, the lady glasses, and lots of ice."

Zuber winked. "A woman who knows what she wants."

"I give orders too."

"I remember." His voice was neutral, his blue eyes weren't, and Ceci gave him a smile that would have melted snow in the Arctic.

"Zuber, why don't you bring menus with the pitcher," Billy said before a live sex act took place before their very eyes.

There was an unnerving pause, then Zuber said, "Right." Giving Ceci a last there's-no-one-here-but-you-and-me look, he reluctantly got to his feet.

An embarrassing spectacle averted, Zuber soon returned with Molly Bee's special punch made with cachaça, her own wild cherry liquor, fresh lime juice, sugar syrup, and bing cherries. The martini glasses were from a Louisiana artist who whimsically used male and female torsos for the glass stems. The glass was molded in a variety of colors, the nude forms were explicit and always a source of conversation. They ordered appetizers. The food was excellent, the drinks cheering, and midway through the pitcher, Serena turned to Frankie. "How old are you?"

Ceci curtailed her narrative of skinny-dipping after the prom long enough to murmur to Serena, "Make an exception."

"Twenty-seven," Frankie replied, looking from Ceci to Serena. "Does it matter?"

Serena had the ability to look sweetly innocent; it came from cajoling favors from her father as a child. "Not in the least," she said lightly. "Do you live around here?"

"Just down the road." He used that calm voice he used with drunks who wanted to fight, the one that gave nothing away.

"On the lake?"

He nodded.

She came to her feet. "Why don't you show me."

He looked up past the flaunting curve of her breasts to her smile and, rising, held out his hand. When she placed her fingers on his palm, he took a small breath, turned to those in the booth and said, "See ya later."

Ceci whispered into Zuber's ear and he began to slide out of the booth. "I guess we're going too," he said, patting his cargo shorts pockets for his keys.

Ceci smiled at Lily. "I'll call you tomorrow."

A moment later, a small silence descended on the corner booth; it had suddenly become an island of quiet in the noisy saloon.

Lily glanced at Billy out of the corner of her eye.

He was smiling at her. "Apparently Zuber and Ceci spend some time together in the summer."

"Apparently." He was easy to smile at. And it wasn't even the drinks.

He shrugged and the muscles across his shoulders rippled under his open-necked T-shirt. "I guess Frankie's had a crush on Serena since dirt."

"I got that impression."

"Ditto here."

"Oh, dear," she murmured, feeling gauche. "I'm sorry. You should have said something to Serena."

"No, I meant you. I used to go to the beach just to see you on the lifeguard tower." He grinned. "The bike ride down wasn't bad, but it was uphill all the way home." His grin widened. "But definitely worth it."

She was surprised at how much better she felt, knowing she, not Serena, was the object of his crush. An expansive rush of pleasure warmed her. "I'm flattered."

His gaze made her clench her fists against a serious jolt of desire.

"Small world," he said, husky and low.

She nodded and tried to speak in a normal tone. "You come home every summer, Ceci tells me." There. That sounded almost normal.

"And you don't. I would have noticed."

"It's been a while." He was half-smiling and she felt curiously comforted, as though they'd known each other in some other life.

"You must have noticed the changes. Espresso everywhere, yoga studios, handmade pottery—"

"But still we have mosquitoes." Fuck. She shouldn't have said that.

He heard the faint bitterness, remembered how his sister used to sound when Dave's name came up. "Sore spot?" His voice was mild.

"My ex hated the mosquitoes and what he called this godforsaken wilderness." Jesus, where did that come from?

Billy's brows rose faintly. "Some people have no appreciation."

"He appreciated other women though." She'd definitely have to stop drinking; she couldn't keep her mouth shut.

"Stupid man."

Lily grimaced. "I was more stupid." She pushed away her drink. "I apologize. This is the last thing in the world I want to talk about."

"Don't beat yourself up," he said. "My sister was

divorced three years ago. She's still not ready to forgive and forget."

Lily's eyes widened. Oh, God. That long?

He'd forgotten how green her eyes were—
Emerald Isle green, upland-pastures-after-a-rain
green, lying-in-bed green, he thought, hungrier
than he'd ever been in his life.

"Take me somewhere," she said abruptly, feeling
as though she were drowning in a tidal wave of
regret.

"Anyplace special?" His voice was extra polite in
contrast to the carnal image front and center in his
brain.

"Someplace with a soft bed. Or are you living at
home? If you are we could go to my—"

"No," he said, pulling some bills out of his
pocket and putting them on the table. "I'm not living at home. And I have—"

"Everything I want."

She was drunk but he didn't care. "I was going
to say a soft bed, but"—he grinned—"thanks. The
feeling's mutual." Sliding out of the booth, he held
out his hand. "Did I tell you I took that lifesaving
course at Shagawa Lake because of you?"

His hand engulfed hers; it was comfortingly
warm, sexy warm. "I wish I'd known it."

"It doesn't matter."

And it no longer did.

CHAPTER 4

He had to move a pile of tools from the floor on the passenger side of the Ace Hardware store truck before she got in. She stood waiting in the quiet of the parking lot, liking how she felt—half lustful, half nostalgic, no longer touched with regret. The air was warm, the sky filled with stars, the northern lights a spectacle of color on the horizon.

"There. Sorry for the mess." Billy held out his hand to help her in. For a man who had to fight off the puck bunnies outside the locker room after every game, for a man who didn't always fight them off, his skittishness was unnerving. He shut her door and walked around the back of the truck, telling himself to get a grip.

"I'm not usually impulsive—like Ceci," Lily said

the minute he opened the door, feeling a sudden need to explain.

"No one's like Ceci. Not that I'd know personally," Billy added quickly. "But she's pretty much out there. Don't worry though. If you hadn't said something, I would have."

"You're sure now? I'm not pushing you or anything?"

He was backing out of the parking space, but he flashed her a look. "Believe me, you're not pushing."

She smiled. "Thanks. The thought just came to me that Ceci sort of set us up and"—her voice trailed away for a moment—"all those ghastly stories of blind dates came to mind. I didn't want you to feel obliged . . . out of politeness"—she shrugged—"or something."

Her breast had moved the merest distance when she'd shrugged and he gripped the steering wheel a little tighter. "I've been talking about you since I saw you in your kitchen this afternoon. Ask Zuber or Frankie. They've been razzing the hell out of me."

She smiled. "It must be karma—not that I believe in it. But I've been obsessing about you since this afternoon. I thought it was the margaritas."

"Thanks," he said dryly.

She touched him then, running her hand down his arm in apology. "I only meant"—she drew in a breath and blew it out again; his muscles were steel hard—"I've never felt like this before. Don't look at me like that." She grinned. "Oh, hell, look at me any way you want. This whole thing is completely out of control."

"And it usually isn't."

"Never."

"No shit. And I believe in karma even less than you do."

"Maybe it *is* the liquor."

"I was sober this afternoon. Hell, I'm sober now."

"I'm not. I hope you don't mind."

"Just for the record, I don't mind one single thing about you. If you pass out, I'll cover you up and watch you sleep."

"I don't want to pass out. I might miss something."

He smiled. "Then we'll see what we can do about keeping you awake." Reaching over, he pulled her close, took both hands off the wheel, framed her face in his hands, and, keeping one eye on the road and his knees on the wheel, kissed her. Sweetly at first and then not so sweetly.

They were both breathing harder when he released her.

"Keep your hands on the wheel," she said on a suffocated breath, thinking how nice it was—feeling as though she was going to die of longing—how strange and curious, how novel. "I'll do the kissing."

He only kept one hand on the wheel. He held her with the other as she twined her arms around his neck and kissed him on his smiling mouth, on his straight nose, on the firm line of his jaw, on his mouth again, longer this time, slower, deeper—no light, brushing kiss now, it was all tongue . . . telling him how much she wanted him.

He groaned deep in his throat and she tasted the sound, his arm tightened on her shoulders and he kissed her back, hard, the promise of sex explicit in each wet thrust of his tongue. The mailboxes along the road swept by, the river bridge, the hill and curve barely noticed, the heat inside the truck cab bringing a sheen to their skin.

Suddenly ravenous, Lily wrenched her mouth away. "Please," she whispered, trying to unfasten his zipper. "Please, please, please . . ."

He pushed her away. "There's not enough room on this seat. Be a good girl"—he exhaled in a great whoosh of air—"and wait a few minutes more."

"Don't want to," she said, pouty and fretful.

He turned to look but she was smiling. "We're almost there," he said, punching the accelerator.

Lily glanced at the road. "You're on the lake too."

"On the point."

"How romantic . . ." Reaching over, she brushed her fingers up his erection.

He lifted her hand away. "Don't."

"That's not very nice." She reached out again.

He caught her wrist before she touched him. "Hold on, babe."

"I'm trying to."

He laughed. "Just a little longer, Miss Lily, and I'll give you—"

"Whatever I want?"

He flashed her a smile. "Yeah . . . in about thirty seconds." Releasing her hand, he hit the brakes and turned onto the Lodge road.

"You live *here*?"

"In the summers."

"We always came for Sunday dinners at the Lodge," she said, intrigued enough to momentarily dismiss her carnal urges. "My *mother* came for Sunday dinners when *she* was a child."

"Same here." Billy gripped the wheel with both hands as the truck skidded around the corner of the old icehouse.

"Do you rent one of the cabins?"

"Sort of." He cranked into what wasn't really a parking spot close to the entrance. Every window was alight; you could hear the band playing in the bar.

A teenage boy ran up to open his door. "Evenin', Billy. The cook has your dinner waitin'."

"Tell her I'll have it later."

"Sure thing, boss."

A moment later, Billy was holding Lily's door open. "Watch your step in the dark." He held out his hand but she didn't move.

"This is yours?"

"Sort of."

"Sort of?"

"Yeah, it's mine." He lifted her from the seat and set her on her feet because short of a nuclear war there was no way he was stopping now. "The path is rough, be careful." He took her hand.

"I don't know if I—" But he was already moving, pulling her along, and her uncertainty failed to clarify into a lucid thought.

He held her hand tightly as he helped her over the tree roots and rocky outcroppings down the path to a large log cabin on the point. The nearly full moon shone above, golden, a faint nimbus surrounding it, the lake reflecting its light in shimmering ripples. The scene was idyllic, like a picture on a calendar.

They walked past the beds of columbine and iris, ascended the broad stairs, crossed a porch with a swing and rockers. Opening the door, he flicked on the light and ushered her into a large room with a stone fireplace covering one wall, two walls of windows facing the lake, and an array of comfortable and colorful furniture, clearly put there by a designer.

Lily stopped just inside the door while Billy moved to open some windows.

Turning back to her a moment later, he said, "What?"

"Why didn't you say something?"

"About what?"

"About this."

"What about it?"

"You own the Lodge?"

"I'm sorry. Is it a problem?"

She leaned back against the door. "You're a celebrity." There. Clarity. She noticed his black linen shorts for the first time, the white T-shirt that fit so smoothly, his leather sandals, all custom-made for a man of his size.

"No I'm not." He moved toward her.

"I'd be going to bed with a celebrity." Who did his hair? she wondered. It had to be cut often to keep that perfect spiky effect.

"Jesus, Lily. I'm just me." He was standing very close, his brows drawn together.

His expensive cologne redolent in her nostrils, she sighed. "It's not your fault." But her tone held stricture. "My ex-husband was a . . . celebrity . . ."

"No one cares about that here. I live a normal life."

"In your"—she gestured around the fabulous room that went with his perfectly tailored clothes—"this . . . this—page out of *Architectural Digest*."

"You're not exactly an unknown either," he countered. "You had your own TV show—I heard about it at the saloon. The number one station in Chicago isn't the hinterlands. Come on." He grinned. "Leave it go."

She tried not to smile but didn't succeed. She hadn't heard that expression for a zillion years. "Damn you." A breathy frustration beneath her smile and then she said in an altogether different voice, "Do I hafta?"

He laughed, pulled her close and ran his palms down her back. "You betcha you do."

Resting her chin on his chest, she gazed up at him, her green eyes coquettish. "You don't sound like a celebrity."

He smiled. "That's because I'm a rayncher to the bone. I work at the hardware store, you know."

How could she take issue with that—or the heat of his palms at the base of her spine? "And I'm going to teach here this year."

"Lucky kids," he murmured.

God, he felt good—hard, muscled . . . ummm, really hard. "I'm thinking I *might* be needing some more repairs at my cabin too."

"Lucky me."

"Right now though," she whispered, rising on tiptoe to brush a kiss across his chin. "I need something else . . ."

"Fer sure." The general statement of agreement in rayncher dialect.

She laughed, a rush of nostalgia enveloping her. Being in his arms was comfort and joy—and bottom-line hot desire like she'd never felt before. Maybe the Molly Bee special cheer-up potion was working its magic. Maybe the pine-scented night air was casting its spell . . . maybe darling Billy was simply very, very hot. Whatever it was, the throbbing between her legs was accelerating with each passing second, and the Rolling Stones lyrics from "Satisfaction" were drowning out more rational thought. "Are you going to show me your bed?"

He nodded. "I was being polite." Because fourteen-year-olds were polite with their fantasies.

"I'm not really in the mood for politeness."

"Are we done with your husband?" he wanted to say, but he wasn't that stupid. "Good," he said instead, lifted her into his arms with an effortless strength and moved toward the bedroom.

A shiver raced up her spine; his sheer power was intoxicating. Who was she kidding? Everything about darling Billy was intoxicating—from the top of his spiky black hair to the bottom of his perfect, tanned feet. Not to mention everything in between—her attention was fixed on one particular location at the moment.

Leaning his shoulder into a door of burled pine, Billy entered a room dominated by a large bed and Lily's reflections on imminent sex were momentarily obliterated by a sense of wonder.

The bed was an awesome creation of birch with facsimile leaves of silk on the branches that soared overhead into a leafy canopy. The coverlet was a white matelassé, tailored, tucked in at the corners; the floor was covered with handwoven rugs in shades of yellow and white.

He felt warm, hot against her, his arms and chest solid, iron-hard, and all she could think of was feeling him inside her.

Billy's feelings were mutual, although perhaps multiplied a couple thousand times by the thirteen years he'd been waiting to do this. Under the circumstances, he was remarkably controlled. It helped that he was sober.

He set her on her feet at the side of the bed and took a restraining breath. Maybe he wasn't that much in control.

Impatient, she reached for the buttons at the

waistband of his shorts and control vanished from the language.

He had her belt unbuckled and slipped free before she had his buttons opened.

He was fast, fast. It was amazing how deft his large fingers were. Her blouse was open in seconds and he slipped it down her arms at the same time as she slid the zipper down on his shorts.

His shorts fell to the floor; he stepped out of them and kicked them aside without looking, his attention fixed on the plump fullness of her breasts. Tossing her shirt aside, he whispered, "Nice," lightly touching her taut nipples through the clinging silk of her chemise. "No bra. You must work out."

"An obsession—of minor importance compared to my current one," she whispered back. "I'm thinking of attacking you."

"No need for that." He pulled his T-shirt over his head. "I surrender." He slid his index fingers under the thin spaghetti straps of her chemise. "Does this go up or down?"

"Up."

She hooked her fingers in the waistband of his boxers. "And these go down."

"Oh, yeah."

She said, "Wow," very softly as his boxers slid down his legs. He was enormous.

He didn't take notice of her response, intent on lifting the filmy silk fabric over the fullness of her breasts. "Raise your arms," he murmured, and she was forced to shift her awestruck gaze.

A second later, he stood with the scrap of fabric between his thumb and fingers, surveying her face—then lower, then back again to her face. "This is unbelievable . . . the chances of this"—his voice was the merest breath of sound—"you and me." He felt the rush of sensation of a hundred past memories coalescing in a split-second documentary in his mind. Him at fourteen. Her beyond his reach.

"I know," she said, her own internal movie reel having to do with all the men she'd known falling short against the sheer physical perfection before her. In the next second, she chided herself for being shallow, but then he began unzipping her shorts and personality defects suddenly became irrelevant.

Only satisfaction became relevant.

Only him putting *that* where she most needed it—deep inside her, although deep didn't look to be an issue.

Quickly stripping off her shorts and underpants, he eased her back against the bed, lifted her onto the crisp white coverlet.

She pulled him down—not that he needed persuasion. Supporting his weight on his arms, he settled between her thighs with a delicacy that belied his 265 pounds—a consequence, perhaps, of his ability to bench-press 300 pounds without breaking a sweat.

When she looked up and smiled, his dark eyes—half-lidded, long-lashed—were only inches away and smiling back.

"This is one of those moments," he murmured, his voice husky and low, teasing and maybe not teasing at all.

"Where have you been all my life?" she whispered, only half in jest herself.

"Waiting for this . . ." Reaching over, he pulled open the bedside table drawer. Rising to his knees, he quickly put on a condom with the speed of considerable practice. And a second after that, his erection was nudging her wetness.

She moved her hips back and forth, lightly upward, and he slid inside her the smallest distance.

She caught her breath and softly moaned.

Tensing his thighs, he cautioned himself to slow down when he didn't want to slow down.

"More . . . more . . ." A breathy heated sound.

And he obliged or partially obliged or obliged as much as he dared, sinking in a tiny bit more.

"Oh, God . . . oh, God . . ."

He felt like praying too, but for patience; his brain was in ramming speed, his cock was so hard it was aching and he was only half-submerged.

She lifted her hips and he eased in another degree. She was wet, wet, silky wet and panting.

He inhaled in constraint and began counting to ten.

Grabbing the back of his head with both hands, she wrenched his face to within inches of hers so he could see the extent of her need. "If I climbed down from my lifeguard tower to feel your cock, darling Billy, I damned well want to feel it all."

"Yes, ma'am," he whispered, his erection swelling at the tantalizing image. "Right away, ma'am." And then he gave her what she wanted, what he wanted, what his throbbing cock and ramming-speed mentality wanted. He flexed his legs and drove in, burying himself to the hilt.

She screamed.

He began to withdraw.

"No! No! No!" she cried, wrapping her legs around his, clutching at his shoulders. "Don't you dare!"

He stopped, pleasure washing over him in waves, his cock completely imbedded in her tight cunt, paradise no longer an abstract concept. Lengthy moments later, when the tumult in his brain had marginally subsided, when she was uttering soft little sighs and he wanted more, he murmured, "I'm going to move now. Don't freak."

"How far?" she said as though they were negotiating missile defense.

"Far enough, but not too far, Miss Greedy."

"Ummm . . . ummm . . . *ummmm* . . ." Distinct intonations of sexual gratification as she met the rhythm of his lower body.

"Any more questions?"

She arched her back, pushed her pelvis upward with a riveting twist of her hips, and the unbridled shock of pleasure jolted through the length of his penis and tore up his spine.

It took him a second to come back to earth.

"Do *you* have any questions?" she murmured, oversweet and dulcet.

"Cute. Are we done now?"

"I certainly hope not."

He laughed. "Should I apologize?"

She gently moved her hips. "I'd rather you do something else to please me."

"Then hold on, Miss Lily," he said with a smile, gripping her hips lightly, his fingers splayed wide to hold her in place. "I'm going to fuck you hard."

She melted around him, his blunt words starkly carnal, the willfulness in those simple words provocative.

He felt her sleek tissue yield, and perversely it gave him pleasure—when he'd never cared about dominance or submission—when he had always considered sex a genial, mutual pleasure. His fingers tightened on her hips and he deliberately plunged deeper.

She gasped.

He held his breath against the raw, acute feeling. Exhaling a moment later, he tried to shake away his hotspur lust. "This might get out of control . . ."

"I don't care." She was shaking, every nerve in her body screaming for release, desire burning through her brain. "I don't care—just hurry."

It was license and excuse and tempting witchery when she said it like that in a velvet voice. Although he didn't need reasons for what he was about to do; he needed a curb on his insanity.

"Please," she whispered. "I'm dying . . ."

He suddenly lost it, plunging into her with a barely suppressed violence. She met him with equal ferocity, her nails digging into his back, and they moved against each other with feverish abandon, each in their own way driven . . . he, by what seemed years of deprivation, she, perhaps too long celibate, impelled by indescribable cravings. She came quickly, her wild scream rising through the silk leaves quivering overhead, echoing through the open windows out onto the moonlit lake. And then she came again because he didn't stop and she was famished and then she came twice more—sobbing at the last from orgasmic overload.

He climaxed after that although he knew even before it was over that he hadn't had enough. "I'm not done yet," he murmured, kissing her lightly before rolling away and sitting up to pull off his condom.

"You're way too good at that," Lily said, watching him swiftly dispose of it.

"Fucking? Thank you, ma'am." He knew very well what she meant, but he wasn't touching that with a ten-foot pole. "And you're damned sweet, Miss Lily," he said with a smile. "Sweet as candy." He rose from the bed. "Don't go away. I'll be right back."

As if she could move, she thought. As if she wanted to with the prospect of his return.

After padding across the room, he shoved open the door to a bathroom with a whole lot of windows, Lily noted, all unshaded, she further noted. He didn't seem concerned and she wondered if part of the attraction of a stay at the Lodge was the glorious nude views of the owner?

She heard water running and before long Billy reappeared carrying a towel and a wet washcloth.

He bowed when he reached the bed. "I'll be your geisha."

"You look much better than any geisha."

"I might argue about who looks better," he said with an admiring gaze. Wiping her crotch with a warm washcloth, he toweled her dry, and climbed back into bed. "Although I do know making love to you was way better than my ninth-grade fantasy. Could I get you something in return—something to eat, a drink, the moon on a platter?"

"A rerun would be nice. If you don't mind—if you don't think me too— Oh!" she squeaked as he settled between her legs, his erection hard against her mons. "I guess you *don't* mind."

"Right now, I'm hoping you don't mind being up all night."

"Only all night . . . ?" she purred.

"I have to work in the morning. Otherwise . . ." He shrugged.

He was way too casual about that *otherwise*. "Fuck you," she muttered, although she knew better even as she spoke and immediately apologized.

He didn't seem concerned. "Tell me what you're pissed about and I'll fix it."

"I had a brief moment of lunacy, that's all."

His brows rose. "Sure? I can fix anything."

I'll bet he could, she thought, which was the problem when it shouldn't be, when she hadn't a right in the world to take issue with his life, sex or otherwise.

"I don't do this all the time if that's what you're thinking." A half-honest statement because he sure as hell didn't get to live his ninth-grade fantasy every night.

A blush crept up her face; was she that transparent? "I wasn't thinking that—I really wasn't," she lied. "Can we change the subject?"

He smiled. "Whatever you want."

A small silence ensued. She didn't know where to look. She felt incredibly gauche for the first time in years.

Taking her chin in his fingers, he lifted it so she had to look into his eyes. "I'm really happy, okay? I'm damned near coming just being with you. So say what's on your mind. Nothing will faze me when I'm on this colossal pink cloud."

She smiled. "I thought this pink cloud thing was just me going over the edge."

"We'll go over the edge together," he said, very softly. "If that's okay with you?"

"I'd like that."

"So, do you want to put the condom on?"

"You *are* a mind reader."

"You're just not deceitful enough. I love it," he added quickly. "Believe me, I do."

"Because women always say the right things to you?"

He shrugged. "It's a dangerous world out there. You learn to be careful."

"You've done this once or twice before."

He shrugged again. "It goes with the territory, which is why I like being home." He moved his hips lightly against her mons, perhaps subconsciously ending a conversation that could turn awkward. "So waddaya say?" His teeth flashed white. "Ready for round two?"

"What if I said no?"

His dark eyes flared wide for the merest second before he shuttered his gaze. "Then we wouldn't do it."

"Would I have to leave?"

He grinned. "Is this a quiz?"

"Yes—no"—she sighed—"no, not at all. It's just my mouth in overdrive."

"Let me put it this way, darling, and I don't as a rule call women 'darling' so give me points for that. I don't want you to leave. I don't think I'd even let you leave. I know, for sure, I don't *want* you to leave because I'd have to get down off my soft pink cloud."

She smiled. "It's definitely a go after that hundred-point answer."

She didn't have to explain further. She let him put on his own condom because she wasn't as adept as he, and after his charming reply, she didn't even care why he was so adept as long as she reaped the benefit of his obviously much practiced finesse.

She was insatiable that night when she'd never been before; sex had always been a pleasure, but not a ravenous gluttony. She apologized for her breathless craving, her unrelenting demands, until he finally put his hand over her mouth and said with a grin, "I've died and gone to heaven. Understand?"

Her level of understanding became crystal clear a few moments later when she experienced the most intense, mind-blowing orgasm of her life. "Definitely heaven," she breathed in its aftermath, hardly able to speak. "Thank you, darling Billy . . ."

When she fell asleep in his arms, sated and content in the wee small hours of the morning, he lay awake, feeling curiously different. The pleasure wasn't so strange, but the contentment was. Normally, he'd be dressed and on his way by now; he disliked polite conversation in the morning. Instead, he found himself watching the coming sunrise with mild disappointment.

That was a first.

Maybe having to be at the store by seven was sanity in disguise.

Then again, maybe he didn't care about being sane.

She stirred in his arms shortly before he was planning to get up and he kissed her awake—sanity be damned.

Her lashes half-lifted, she lazily arched her back and smiled. "You look familiar . . ."

"You look good enough to—"

"Fuck?"

"To eat, I was going to say . . ."

She grinned. "That'll work."

The alarm clock suddenly emitted an ear-piercing screech.

Swearing, Billy threw a pillow at it, silencing it.

"I like that," Lily murmured. "A man of action."

"Unfortunately, also one of haste. Feel free to say no."

"Work?"

Even as he nodded, he was mentally readjusting his timetable.

"It wouldn't take long," she whispered. Sleep hadn't reduced the level of her lust, and if she weren't so carnally motivated, she might have had time to question her unprecedented obsession.

"It never does with you."

Her green eyes were amused. "Complaining?"

"Not on your life."

It turned out not to be so hasty after all because Billy made a phone call about six-thirty. Someone else could open the store that morning, he decided—a sensible solution considering they didn't come up for air until nearly ten, at which point he rolled over on his back and said, "I'm hungry."

"Is that different?" she replied, gazing at him with a smile.

"Smartass. For food."

She made a face. "Rejected for a plate of flapjacks."

"I think I'll just lock you in until I come back from work. Is that committed enough?"

A sudden silence fell as though a bomb had dropped.

And then they both started to talk at once.

"You first," he said, but he was already climbing out of bed.

"I just wanted to say thank you," Lily noted with what she hoped was a voice of calm. "And I can walk home from here."

He turned when he reached the bathroom door. "I could have some food sent down for you. But I *do* have to get to work."

"Don't bother. I'm not hungry."

The adjective hung in the air, reminding them of appetites that had nothing to do with food—of all that had passed between them in the heated hours of the night.

"Fine." His voice was mild, his smile polite. Then he walked into the bathroom and shut the door.

She was gone when he came out.

He told himself he was relieved, but he was strangely restless as he drove to the store.

CHAPTER 5

Zuber and Ceci had been up all night, but then they were both more familiar with sex as sport. They were also more familiar with each other. So when Zuber kissed her with a gentle, lingering kiss, Ceci knew he was leaving.

"How long will you be gone?"

He rolled away and sat up. "Three days, maybe four." Glancing back over his shoulder, he smiled. "So if you can't be good, be careful."

Her smile reflected her satisfaction as she stretched lazily. "Back at you."

"Unless I'm going to copulate with the CEO and assorted male sundry of Consolidated Electric, it's highly unlikely this will be a sexually oriented trip."

"I'm relieved."

"I wish I could say the same, but I doubt you'll be leaving a light in the window for me."

"Do you want me to?"

He didn't answer right away; he rose from the bed, walked over to where he'd left his shorts in a pile on the floor and picked them up. "Good question."

"I'm not sure that's an answer."

"I'm thinking." He stepped into his boxers, then his cargo shorts, and zipped them up.

He looked tanned and lean, splendidly muscled; he'd pulled his dark hair behind his ears and his cheekbones revealed his Serbian ancestry. Ceci shrugged off a rare sense of loss. "Look, darling," she said, conscious of his nonanswer, aware of her own preferences as well. "A fuck is a fuck is a fuck. Let's not complicate things."

He was picking up his shirt and he stopped, his gaze narrowing for a second before he stood upright. "Suit yourself."

"I usually do."

"Are we fighting?"

"Why should we fight?"

He shrugged. "Beats me." He pulled his T-shirt over his head and shoved in his arms. "Wanna go steady?" he said with a grin.

"Hell, no."

He wiped imaginary sweat from his forehead, and walking over to the bed where she lay in nude splendor, he placed his hands on both sides of her head, leaned close, and kissed her very, very softly. "You're my best girl, Cignoli, I swear."

"And you're worth staying up with all night, Zuber."

He grinned. "What God hath joined . . ."

She hit him, but he didn't even flinch. He licked the tip of her nose and lazily smiled. "I'll be back in three days—four at the most—unless those dudes from the city can't catch the fish I bring them to. So you be ready for my return, 'cause I'm going to be real horny after three days without you."

"How horny?"

"The-way-you-like-it horny. All night and every which way."

Her brows rose faintly. "I think it's your suave charm that most appeals to me."

"I know what most appeals to you," he said, rising, "and I've never heard it called 'charm' before." He blew her a kiss. "See ya, Cignoli. And don't tell your friends every last effing detail."

"But they want to know."

He groaned.

"It's the way we bond," she said with a grin. "You know, like you guys talk about the women you nailed."

He was halfway to the door and he turned. "I never even told them about you."

As the door closed on him, Ceci's mouth was still agape.

CHAPTER **6**

The women were sitting at a corner table in the
Chocolate Moose, having lunch.

Serena was looking all dewy eyed and flushed
and she hadn't stopped talking since they'd arrived.
"I mean, I *really* think I'm in love."

Lily and Ceci were nearly speechless, although
they'd been responding as best they could considering Serena had never understood the accepted
definition of love. Getting money and expensive
gifts from boyfriends wasn't what the world at large
viewed as love.

"He doesn't have a penny," Serena said, not for
the first time, as though trying to get used to the
idea that something so bizarre could actually occur
in her world. "Well, not exactly, I suppose, because
he has to make *something* if he's the county sheriff.

But I mean that's not really *money*. That's some pittance, like what teachers make—No offense, Lily, I know you're only doing this for a year and then going back to your fabulous TV salary. He can't even buy me jewelry," she declared in the serious tone in which someone else might have said, "Global warming is going to devastate the world's food sources in five years." She suddenly smiled. "But he's fabulous in bed. Did I tell you that?" She gazed at her friends with a look of wonder.

They both nodded, as they had the last ten times she'd asked them and then they both said, "Isn't that great!" for the tenth time.

But she wasn't really listening to anyone but herself; Serena didn't as a rule.

"And he talks!" Serena exclaimed. "Just wonderfully, about all kinds of things."

She hadn't said that before.

"What about?" Ceci and Lily said simultaneously, intrigued because Frankie didn't own any diamond mines or yachts he could talk about.

"He told me about his family; he has eight brothers and sisters. Can you imagine? And simply dozens of cousins and aunts and uncles. I can't begin to understand what it's like, but it sounds delightful."

Ceci and Lily exchanged startled looks. Serena was an only child who found it difficult to visit her mother and father more than once every five years.

"He's going to pick me up at the Birch Lake Saloon tonight because he has some crisis at work that will make him late. I said I'd be there with you!" Serena bestowed her I've-never-been-so-happy smile on her friends.

Ceci took a bite of her muffin and said through it, "If I go."

"I'm not sure I will either," Lily replied, reluctant to risk running into Billy after the awkwardness this morning.

Quickly swallowing, Ceci swung her gaze toward Lily. "Trouble in paradise?"

"Sort of." Lily pursed her lips faintly. "Not that I had any illusions, mind you. Nor do I want you to get involved," she added firmly. "Understand?"

Ceci threw up her hands. "I swear, no involvement; I'll be as uninvolved as a nun with a dildo, although maybe that's not a good example, but you know what I mean. What happened?"

"To begin with—there really is a paradise," Lily said with a smile. "But, then, with morning—" Her expression changed.

"Came the usual male retreat," Ceci bluntly finished.

"I don't know about usual. I'm not as dedicated to the sport of love as you. But certainly, this morning, darling Billy took a scare."

"Did you say something?"

"Actually, no, he did. The word *commitment* accidentally came up . . . just in passing. You'd think I'd said I was moving in. He closed down completely."

Ceci laughed. Even Serena smiled, having had

her own experience with the dreaded word. "And?" Ceci said.

"And he went all glassy-eyed, like 'Do I know you?,' made some bland excuse about having to go to work, walked into the bathroom, and shut the door. I was grateful to be able to leave without having to face him again."

"But up until that point was paradise up to your standards?"

Lily couldn't stop from grinning. "It was quite exceptional."

"Then he'll be back."

"Maybe I don't want him back."

"He'll be back anyway, mark my words."

"We'll see if I give a damn. I'm not sure I'm interested in a man who goes from 'I can't get enough of you' to a blank stare in a split second. I practically got whiplash. So, tell me, was *your* night as eventful? You and Zuber seemed to be good friends."

"The very best of friends," Ceci said softly. "And he would prefer me not to give you a blow by blow."

"So?"

"So maybe I won't."

"God Almighty," Lily exclaimed. "I'm surrounded by lovesick women."

"I'm not lovesick," Ceci protested.

"I am," Serena said proudly. "It's very, very nice. And maybe Billy will change his mind and we can all go to the Birch Lake Saloon tonight and have that nice cheer-up potion that makes one feel so pleasant. Even Frankie likes it. Say you'll come. We haven't been home together in ages and I'm having fun."

"I'll see," Lily said evasively.

Serena grimaced. "That's not very nice when I want us all to be together."

"I'll probably go," Lily amended.

"You'll go, won't you, Ceci?" Serena insisted.

"Sure. Okay."

"There, Lily, you're the only spoilsport," Serena pronounced. "Say you'll come too."

She would have preferred not to, but Serena looked so hopeful, Lily didn't have the heart to refuse. "Just for a little while," she said.

CHAPTER 7

Lily decided she'd drive tonight because she wanted to make sure she had a means of escape should Ceci and Serena's interests be other than hers. She had every intention of staying for a short time and then leaving. It wasn't that she was a coward and unwilling to meet Billy in public. She could do that just fine—but she'd prefer an intermission of a day or two to make sure she could be suitably casual.

She'd had time once she returned to her cabin after lunch not only to take a nap after her sleepless night, but to give herself a good talking-to. That internal monologue centered on her immediate goals, her long-term goals, and the fact that no one-night stand was going to wreck her peace of mind. She'd come to Ely this year to get over the anguish of her divorce, to get away from men like Brock who couldn't be trusted, and she didn't intend to get involved with another man who had to beat women off with a stick.

It would be damned foolish to become frustrated by something as inconsequential as Billy Bianchich's take on women. She was on sabbatical from a marriage gone bad, from a life that had become too whirlwind, and what she needed was tranquility, not another disappointing relationship. Although in all honesty, the word *disappointing* only pertained to the last three minutes she'd been with Billy.

The ten hours before had been damned near perfect. She smiled. Okay, perfect.

So she really had no cause to complain.

She was in relatively good spirits as she dressed for the evening. The summer evening was superb—warm with the lingering sunset of the northern latitudes in June—all lush and golden and ethereal. She put on a short swingy black-and-white polka-dot skirt, strappy sandals, and a black tube top decorated with jet beads—one of her outfits from her rooftop TV garden show, *Lily's Garden*. The studio execs liked her in summer dresses, although they said it was the viewers. Since it was part of the show's budget, it didn't matter to her who liked what: sundresses, shorts, decorated jeans, and T-shirts; she had a closetful. The station was airing *The Best of Lily's Garden* reruns to keep her job open for her too, or so they said, but then another blond botanist might come down the pike next week and they'd forget Lily's name. If, however, the pike was still empty of competition next year when her teaching contract at the community college was over *and* if she didn't mind rubbing shoulders with her ex and his new girlfriend/coanchor, she might take the station up on its offer.

Ceci had walked over before Lily was ready and lay on her bed asking questions while she finished dressing. "If you don't want to divulge the details of your evening," Lily noted with a smile, "I'm not inclined to tell you how big Billy is. So stop asking."

Ceci grinned. "You can't fault a girl for trying."

"Feel free to find out for yourself. I'm sure darling Billy is available."

"Do I detect a bit of pique?"

"Not in the least. Let's be practical. I spent one night with him. I'm sure that puts me on a very long list."

"And you're not looking for a repeat?"

Lily snapped on a wide jet bracelet. "I came up here to get away. Not to take on more problems. Peace and tranquility—that's my mantra." She grinned. "Or at least until I feel like hot sex again. Although after last night, I can afford to be celibate for quite some time."

"Sure you won't be tempted?"

Lily shook her head. "Not by him. Really. The last thing I need is some man who's going to lock himself in the bathroom when the word *commitment* comes up. Now, unless you stop pestering me about Billy Bianchich, I'm going to tell Zuber next time I see him that you told me everything—including how big his dick is."

Ceci sat up and came to her feet. "My lips are sealed."

"It must be love."

"I don't know about that, but it's damned fine sex. Let's leave the love stuff for Serena."

"Amen to that."

Serena hadn't come down from her happy place yet and the conversation at the saloon consisted primarily of the variety of ways in which Frankie Aronson was special. The bar was busy; it was Friday and the tourists were arriving for the weekend or their long-planned vacations in the Boundary Waters. Ely was the jumping-off point for the wilderness area, and whether you liked to rough it on your canoe trip with martinis and a steak or Budweiser and canned beans, this was the place where your journey into the vast lake country began.

The Siminich brothers who owned the saloon had live music in the summer and tonight a rocking band was keeping the decibel levels high. Ceci seemed to know everyone, and as they sat in their booth drinking Molly Bee's potion, people kept stopping by. Some Lily knew, most she didn't; the town had changed a lot in thirteen years. It wasn't a sleepy mining town any longer; it was boutiquey and semihip, filled with BMW convertibles and Volvo station wagons, with ex-lawyers and ex-brokers who were living off their bank accounts, enjoying the beauties of nature and keeping in touch with the outside world via fax machine and e-mail.

The Siminiches were making the rounds, diet Cokes in hand, greeting their patrons with the casual cheer that went with their laid-back, ganja lifestyle. Only a year apart, they looked like twins in their Hawaiian shirts and dreadlocks. Known affectionately as the Rastafarian brotherhood by the locals, their illegal propensities were tolerated—along with their questionable fly-in business that serviced the outpost camps on the Canadian border—because they were universally kind and contributed generously to the local charities.

"Girls' night out?" Les said as the brothers stopped at their booth.

"Zuber must be out in the bush," Larry remarked, looking at Ceci.

"Yeah. Lily and I are stag. Serena's waiting for Frankie."

Les winked at Lily, a slow-motion wink that went with his slow-mo view of the world. "Caught your show once in Chicago. Bet your male audience numbers were sky-high."

"Chauvinist pig," Ceci said with a grin.

"Hell, I went out and bought a hydrangea the next day. Don't knock it."

"Good to have you back in town." Larry smiled

at Lily. "Good to have you *all* back in town," he added, his gaze swinging to Ceci and Serena. "You three really dress up the place."

Les lifted his can of diet Coke. "Anything we can do for you ladies, just say the word." Then they strolled off to schmooze with the patrons in the next booth.

Lily smiled. "They haven't changed in thirteen years."

"They're just a little richer now," Ceci said.

Gazing around the large space, Lily took note of the booths overflowing with people, the three-deep crowd at the bar, the dance floor awash with dancers.

"They didn't even have a paper route when I knew them."

"They went off to college in Duluth and took a fancy to Internet stocks. They were very focused, I hear. Maybe it was the weed. Or maybe it was their flying skills—bush pilots from the cradle, those Siminiches—that moved them into the high-profit entrepreneurial ranks. Anyway, they made a bundle one way or another, they always wanted a bar—go figure—and when the saloon came up for sale when Lloyd retired . . ." Ceci waved her arm in the direction of the crowded room. "There you have it—another tribute to hard work and clean living in the good ol' U.S. of A."

"It hasn't gone to their heads. They're still incredibly nice."

"Like Frankie." It had been over five minutes

since Serena had had the opportunity to praise her favorite person. "He's incredibly nice too." Her bottom lip pushed out a little. "I wish he didn't have to take care of his silly work crisis. I wish he were here *right* now."

"He'll be here soon, and then you can have him for the rest of the night," Ceci soothed.

"You know, I'm really glad we had our little talk yesterday or I may never have decided to go out with younger men." Serena's baby-blue eyes went all wide and tickled-pink-delighted. "Younger men are *so* much better!"

"Can't say I have any complaints," Ceci said, her smile sort of far away and wistful.

"You two are going to make me lose my supper, although I mean that in the nicest way," Lily said with a smile.

"Just because you didn't find someone as wonderful as Frankie—oh, dear, I'm sorry, Lily." Even Serena, who didn't focus outside herself often, took note of Lily's embarrassment. "Probably hockey players aren't very nice. Don't they hit each other with their sticks all the time? A man like that isn't going to be—well . . . very nice. Just forget him, like I did Homer," she said firmly.

"I already have."

"Good. Good for you. It's all about taking personal responsibility and being positive and having affection for yourself—they were talking about that on *Oprah* today. Although the psychologist who was explaining about being positive said something rude about his wife so it didn't seem like he was taking his own advice. But I'm sure it's a very good idea in theory."

Maybe it was and maybe it wasn't, but the theory was about to be tested because Frankie had just walked through the door and he wasn't alone.

Lily was surprised at the sudden heat that flared through her body. Then she was irritated. She'd be damned if Billy Bianchich was going to make her hot! Quickly coming to her feet, she said, "I'm going to the ladies' room. I'll be right back."

Serena was waving like the last survivor of a life raft trying to get the attention of a passing freighter.

"Are you coming back?" Ceci asked Lily in an undertone.

"Of course."

Although Lily seriously considered decamping when she exited the bathroom some time later and both men were seated at their booth. But long before the current wave of reaffirming quasi-religion had overtaken the culture, she'd had a pretty good sense of herself. There was no way she was going to let a man intimidate her.

Her smile in place, she approached the group, uttered all the usual polite greetings, and sat down next to Ceci.

Billy had caught sight of Lily the minute he'd walked into the bar; he'd seen her leave the booth, had watched her return, sheer willpower keeping him seated as she neared. She was half-undressed in that strapless top and short, bouncy skirt, her long blonde hair in soft waves on her bare shoulders, and he remembered how her skin felt, how silky soft it was, how soft it was everywhere. He shifted in his chair to accommodate his rising erection and swore under his breath.

He didn't like feeling this way—tormented, hungry. He didn't want to want a woman this much; he never had. Jesus, she smelled good. The familiar scent of her perfume drifted across the table and all he could think of was carrying her out of the bar and making love to her the minute they were beyond the range of the porch lights. Although in his current mood, even the porch lights weren't a serious problem.

She wouldn't look at him though, so sex was probably out.

The band started playing a loud, fast rendition of "Brown Sugar" by the Stones, and Frankie and Serena got up to dance.

An awkward silence fell.

"You're the garden lady from Chicago!" A preppy-looking, fair-haired man was smiling at Lily. "I told Bob it was you! Care to dance?"

Billy glared at the obvious tourist in his Dockers and moccasin loafers. "She's with me."

"I'm not with him." Lily shot Billy an annoyed look. "I'd love to dance," she said sweetly.

For a split second, Billy debated making a scene and his expression must have shown it.

"Don't," Ceci said, sotto voce.

"Don't you dare," Lily hissed. Turning to the man in the Dockers, she offered him a radiant smile, slipped her arm through his, and walked away.

Billy came halfway out of his chair at the word *dare* but Ceci pulled him back. "Steady, Bianchich. You do that, you have to do more," she warned him. "Think of that."

He settled back. But he followed Lily with his gaze.

"She doesn't need you to mess with her head. She just got rid of an asshole," Ceci said sharply.

He inhaled deeply. "Right." He turned back and glanced around as though he'd just walked out of a cave after a year. "Busy tonight," he said. "Howya doin'?"

"Welcome to the world," Ceci said sardonically. "Had your mind somewhere else, did you?"

He blew out a breath. "Fuck . . ."

"When you do that, take my advice, pick on someone who doesn't want to remember your name in the morning."

"And who the hell would that be?"

"Sorry, Mr. Big Shot. I guess they all want a piece of your star-studded ass."

"Sorry, Ceci," he said with genuine humility. "Lily really got to me."

"And you don't know what to do because no one ever has before."

"Same as you."

"Maybe."

His gaze took on a new directness. "Don't tell me the lady who prides herself on her independence might be softening up?"

"Maybe," she repeated, her expression bland.

"Care to elaborate?" They'd become friends of sorts in the past few summers, meeting often at various functions, bars, parties.

"No."

"Don't want to scare off Zuber?"

"Now there's a man talking. Maybe I don't want to scare off myself."

"Sorry. It's in the blood—that fear of—"

"Lily said the word was *commitment* this morning," Ceci said with a smile.

He jerked back in his chair as though recoiling from an assailant.

She laughed. "Good luck, Bianchich, you're going to need it. And speaking of luck, look who's coming your way. The easiest lay in town."

A moment later, Tammy Connors leaned over, slid her arms around Billy's shoulders from behind, and whispered something in his ear.

He didn't respond for a three count and then he turned and smiled at her. "Why not," he said, coming to his feet.

Sometimes God sent you a sign.

CHAPTER **8**

O nce Billy walked out of the bar with the
    black-haired bitch, as Lily silently referred to
his partner, she found it easier to enjoy the rest of
the evening. His disappearance resolved her
dilemma—should she, shouldn't she, would she
hate herself in the morning if she did? It turned
into a beautiful, hot, sweaty night of dancing,
which she loved. The band was prime, she adored
dancing, she had no dearth of partners, including
Ceci whom she'd danced with since the sixth grade.
They were actually damned good.

Serena and Frankie left early. Surprise, surprise.
But it was nice to see Serena so happy.

After turning down various offers to extend the
evening, Lily and Ceci drove home alone.

"Is it just me or do you have to feel the heat before you sleep with someone?" Lily asked as they turned out of the saloon parking lot.

"Same here. Lust first, then friendship. That's my motto."

"There's definitely degrees of lust though." Lily sighed.

"He talked about you," Ceci said, the reason for Lily's sigh patently clear.

"But he went home with the black-haired bitch."

"It was a without-risk, try-to-forget-the-woman-you-want fuck. He would have preferred you, but didn't want to pay the price."

"That's not particularly consoling."

"But true. He wants you bad."

Even while she told herself she shouldn't care, even while she understood how useless the feeling was, Lily felt a warm rush of pleasure.

Lily was home twenty minutes later, still wired after the hours of dancing. Taking off her clothes, she put on a robe, poured herself a Coke from the refrigerator, opened and shut the bag from the Chocolate Moose with the almond-paste bear claw three times before she decided she'd burned off enough calories on the dance floor to warrant a tiny little bite.

Three minutes later the bear claw was gone.

She'd only eat raw vegetables tomorrow, she promised herself, and then in some totally unknown fashion, the freezer door was open, she was standing in the glare of the freezer light, and the Ben & Jerry's Cherry Garcia container was looking lonely all by itself.

She'd eat only a very *few* raw vegetables tomorrow, she thought, reaching for it.

Scooping up the first spoonful—the one with the large chocolate chunk—she mentally considered eating just down an inch, reassuring herself that calculating the number of fat grams and calories listed in a portion size when divided by the very few spoonfuls she would consume would only amount to a nominal number of calories. And a certain amount of fat was actually required in the diet or one could die of beriberi or some similar, odd disease of malnutrition.

She was shocked when she saw the bottom of the container.

Tomorrow would have to be a day of fasting, which was very good for one; it cleansed one's soul and body and allowed one to reach a higher sphere of consciousness.

With *tomorrow* the operative word, she drank her Coke and then finished off that one last small Almond Joy left over from her trip. The Almond Joys were really much, much smaller than before— a mere morsel with hardly any calories, she was sure. And she'd read somewhere that coconut didn't have any cholesterol, although the palm oils weren't all that good for you, but she wasn't going to think about that now—*when she was in the throes of a severe case of sexual deprivation!*

She chose to overlook the fact that she'd gone two months without sex prior to arriving in Ely.

But too much factual data put you out of touch with your true inner self and the cosmic energy cycles that brought you extraordinary peace and understanding. So right now, she didn't want to be confused with *petty* facts. She was much more interested in *where he went with that black-haired bitch!*

Calm, calm . . . draw in a breath of serenity and peace . . . let your vital life energy flow . . .

Lily picked up the kitchen phone.

Ten minutes later, Ceci had talked her down: she wasn't going to weigh three hundred pounds by next week due to her sexual trauma; all she needed was a good night's sleep and everything would look calm and much improved in the morning. One thought less often of ex-lovers making love to black-haired bitches, she supposed, when one was eating her scrambled eggs and toast than when one was perhaps just *slightly* drunk.

A glaring light flashed through the kitchen windows, and for a second she thought she'd witnessed an alien landing.

It was car lights, she realized a moment later. She really shouldn't have more than three drinks in an evening.

The headlights were turned off, she heard a car door slam, and it just went to show you how harmful violence in movies was, because her first thought was that someone had come to cut her into ribbons with a kitchen knife in, appropriately, her kitchen.

The part of her brain that hadn't been completely blunted by alcohol reminded her that no one had been cut to ribbons in Ely—ever. That momentarily calming reminder allowed her to flash forward to a less vicious but equally alarming scenario about a woman who was attacked in her kitchen by a huge flock of birds. The lucid part of her brain screamed: STUPID! BIRDS DON'T DRIVE CARS!

Nevertheless, the knock on the door sent a small shiver up her spine.

"Yes?" she said, so softly even she realized no one could hear it. Clearing her throat for a second attempt, she glanced about, hoping to catch sight of a large-bladed kitchen knife within easy grasp. But since she hadn't cooked since her arrival, nor had she opened a drawer save to find the spoon she needed to finish the Cherry Garcia, she knew it wasn't likely that a useful long-bladed weapon would be readily available.

"Lily! I can hear you breathing in there. Open the door."

Was that a choir of angels that had raised their voices on high or was she hallucinating after only five or six or at the very most seven drinks at the Birch Lake Saloon?

"Lily, dammit. Open the door or I'll break it down."

The angels stopped singing at Billy's rather harsh tone of voice. "Don't shout!" she shouted.

"Open the door," he said in a near normal tone.

"It's not locked."

She could hear him swearing and a second later he was standing in her kitchen looking just as good as he had earlier—maybe better now that she was in harmony with her inner self and her spontaneous and wholly natural sexual impulses. Peace and tranquility—that was the answer.

"Where's that black-haired bitch you left with?" Her spitefulness surprised her, coming out without warning, but then the secrets of cosmic understanding require years of disciplined study. She'd start first thing in the morning.

"I don't know," he said, smiling, like he knew something she didn't; she wondered if her robe was undone. "Do you want to go and look for her?"

"Why would I want to do that?"

"Ceci said you wanted to strangle her."

"Ceci's an unspeakable traitor—like an Aaron Burr or was it Nathan Hale? Who sold his country for—"

"I'm glad she called me."

The way he said it sent a small shiver the other way this time, downward. "You are?"

"I am."

"Would you care to explain?"

"Not really."

"I suppose the word *commitment* mustn't be uttered on pain of death."

"I suppose I'd better make you some coffee or you're not going to remember a thing in the morning."

"I don't care about commitment," she meant to say, but it came out slurred and the word *commitment* took three tries.

He didn't seem to notice. He walked from the kitchen door around the table in the center of the floor to the counter where she was half standing and half leaning and listening to the choir of angels. He took her in his arms, looked into her eyes, and said, very, very softly, "I know. It was my fault. Now, where's your coffee?"

CHAPTER **9**

At the same time just down the road, a utilitarian Range Rover, dull finish green, high bumpers with winches front and rear, ground in low gear up the steep driveway to Ceci's cabin. Although the cabin was dark, the driver didn't hesitate to walk up to the back door and let himself in. He moved through the shadowed kitchen and living room, out onto the screened porch. Standing at the foot of the daybed where Ceci slept, he smiled faintly.

Then he began undressing, dropping his clothes on the green-painted floor. Ceci lay facedown, a quilt pulled up to her ears against the coolness of the night. The moonlight picked up the blondeness in her tawny hair, it bathed her right cheek with liquid silver, streaked her bare arm that lay near her face on the pillow.

He was bone tired, but it was worth it, the man thought, moving forward.

"Hey!" Half-asleep, Ceci brushed away the finger that touched her cheek.

The bed dipped and her eyes snapped open.

"Hey, back," Zuber whispered, sliding under the quilt and pulling her into his arms.

"Did I sleep through the week?" Ceci muttered, her brain racing through a chronology that wasn't working out. Although Molly Bee's potion could have something to do with the "not working out."

"Six satellite phones went crazy about halfway up Knife Lake. Every one of the Consolidated Electric dudes was talking as fast as he could. Some hostile takeover, apparently. So we turned around."

"You came through the lakes at night?"

"Had to. I could do it blindfolded anyway. Besides, I knew you'd be here."

She was awake now, feeling partly all warm and fuzzy and partly annoyed. "I hope you're not taking me for granted."

"Hell, no, I just figured I'd find you no matter who you were with and drag you home."

"What if I didn't want to be dragged home?"

"Didn't think of that."

"And what if the guy I was with took issue?"

"Didn't care."

"One-track-mind Zuber."

"How about a little appreciation? I've been on the lakes since seven this morning. I busted my butt over five portages and through six lakes to get back here."

"Because Consolidated Electric was being taken over."

"Because I had a chance to come back early. Do I give a damn about six guys I never saw before and I'll never see again? By the way, they can't paddle worth a damn. Buster, Scotty, and I literally manhandled their sorry asses up and down those lakes."

"Really, you did it for me?" The warm fuzzies were back big time.

"Yeah. So don't give me any grief."

"I turned down three invitations for, shall we say, a sleepover tonight. How's that?"

"Lucky me."

And then he kissed her, and when he was done kissing her, she didn't much feel like talking anymore.

"If I fall asleep, you have my permission to kick me awake," he whispered, dipping his head to lick one of her nipples. "Although that's not likely to happen in the next five minutes."

His erection was rock-hard against her thigh and he was gently sucking her nipple so little heated waves were rolling downward, making her wet and hot. Hot like a two-month summer drought in Alabama, or more to the point, hot like she hadn't had Zuber inside her since this morning. She slid her fingers through his hair and pulled his head up. "Do you mind?" Her voice was strangely breathless . . . or not so strangely, considering it was Zuber's cock rubbing her leg. "I'm a couple hundred miles past foreplay right now."

His grin flashed white in the moonlight and he reached for one of the condoms. "Ask me why I'm not surprised."

"I don't need sarcasm right now. I need—"

"This," he said.

Lord, he was fast—all raw muscle and supple strength—and then she lost track of his glorious attributes save for his most glorious one that was gliding in slowly, filling her slowly, making her a true believer in cosmic bliss.

When he was in so deep he couldn't go any deeper, he arched his back against the riveting sensation and softly groaned.

Welcome home, Ceci thought, liking the sound he made low in his throat, the way he made her feel as though she were floating in some torrid equator-like zone of sensation where pleasure was nearly within grasp.

She moved her hips faintly, reaching for the brass ring.

He moved slightly back and upward.

And they both caught their breaths.

He knew what she liked or maybe what all women liked, she thought, not with prejudice, but with gratitude because he'd withdrawn with the same lingering restraint as he'd entered her and she held her breath waiting for his downstroke.

There, there—there . . . Oh, God . . .

Reeling, she screamed—a little feverish, panting scream.

And he was damned glad his arms had held out long enough to paddle home.

The rhythm of their bodies quickened, a foment of frenzy and delirium took over, and well matched in their prodigality, knowing there was more, they both took the short route to paradise.

Moments later, their first ravenous hunger sated, they lay in each other's arms, rapture dissolving away by slow degrees.

"I should thank whoever was taking over that electric company," Ceci said, stretching up to lightly kiss Zuber's cheek.

He glanced down and smiled. "I already did."

"You can stay then—I mean—oh, hell . . ."

"Hey, I'm staying."

"Good." She couldn't help but smile.

"It always *is* good with you. I must like poets."

"I wrote a poem about you today. Wanna hear it?"

"Do I have a choice?"

She socked him. He grinned and said, "Did I mention how I was hoping you'd read me a poem?"

"You almost had your nooky ration taken away."

"Yeah, right."

"You think I can't go without it?"

"I *know* you can't go without it."

"You're not exactly a monk yourself."

"Why do you think we get along so well?"

She batted her eyelashes at him. "Because we both like poetry."

He laughed. "Read me the damned poem."

But when she returned to the bed with her notebook, he'd fallen asleep, and she stood for a moment watching the gentle rise and fall of his chest. In some ways, she liked the intensity of her feelings for him. In other ways, she didn't. It wouldn't pay to become too enamored of a man like Nick who had a fresh crop of pursuing women each summer. While those in his past didn't forget him either. She cautioned herself as she had last summer and the summer before—not to become involved. It was about sex. It wasn't about anything else.

Setting her notebook on the table, she gently eased back into bed. He'd had a long, hard day. She would have dropped dead if she'd had to paddle a canoe for an hour, let alone all the way up to Knife Lake and back.

He came awake as the warmth of her body touched his. "Sorry," he said, forcing his eyes open. "Sorry about that."

Leaning over, she kissed him. "Go back to sleep. I'll see you in the morning."

"I'm awake," he said, his voice still drowsy. "Give me a minute . . ."

With the determination that probably accounted for so many of his racing records, she watched him pull himself back into consciousness. "You don't have to be polite for me," she offered. "I can wait."

He ran his fingers through his hair, gently shook his head. "What's on the agenda?"

"Oh, I don't know—I thought maybe we'd check out the news on CNN."

He grinned. "Or we could check out this hot poet I know," he said, rolling on his side and pushing her legs apart with the palm of his hand. "Ummm, smooth . . ."

"Unlike your hand," she murmured, his callused palm sending little shivers through her, his I-can-take-care-of-myself-in-the-wilderness maleness arousing her at the most primitive level. Me Tarzan, you Jane, primordial lust washed over her and she rose into the two strong fingers he slipped up her vagina.

His touch was remarkably delicate, his competence like so many of his skills expert. Soon, she was squirming, begging for more. He moved between her legs, replaced his fingers with his mouth and tongue and addressed himself to her clitoris.

She'd forgotten—how could she have in less than a day?—how that exquisite degree of tactile sensation shocked and jolted and brought one to shrieking orgasm. Perhaps that lack of memory was a survival mechanism so one didn't do it too often and expire from hysteria.

The light, deft pressure of his tongue sent exquisite vibrations, hot, deep throbbing beats, upward and outward in blissful waves, molten pleasure stretching through her vagina, flooding her senses, sliding up her spine in a pure self-centered, all-consuming ache. With a low moan, she moved against his mouth, half hungry, half inundated in a roseate bliss. Sliding her fingers through his hair, she drew him closer, ravenous, tantalized, wet with wanting, and his tongue glided in deeper. With his upper lip lodged against her turgid clitoris, he curled the tip of his tongue against the front wall of her vagina, and gently licked her G-spot in a slow, exacting rhythm that quickly brought her to a state of panting arousal. Within seconds, she came in a high, breathy scream, and even before the last orgasmic ripples died away, he touched her . . . there . . . again and she felt the flooding pleasure build anew.

He didn't stop until she'd come an outrageous number of times.

She was gasping when it was over.

Easing her fingers from his hair, he raised himself on his elbows.

When she opened her eyes and looked down, he was smiling at her. "I'm pretty well awake now."

"Did I scream?"

"What?" Grinning, he put his hand to his ear.

She put her foot to his shoulder and he rolled away. Sitting up, he leaned back against the porch wall and beckoned with one finger. "Come here."

"Why?"

"It's my turn, that's why."

But it wasn't exclusively, because he lifted her onto his lap, eased her down his erection, and holding her captive with his hands on her hips, gently kissed her until she whimpered and cried and finally came without moving. And then he raised her with an effortless strength and lowered her again in a slow, languorous rhythm, stopping each time at the ultimate depth of penetration so they could both feel the feverish heat, so the need for surcease almost—almost—peaked. But not quite; he knew precisely how to balance delay and hovering desire.

Until she swore at him and bit his lip and threatened to do him bodily harm.

He smiled, eased his hands from her hips, and let her ride him to consummation. Patience had never been Ceci's forte.

But even lust and courtesy eventually succumbed to weariness and hours later he collapsed on his back, arms stretched wide. "I'm sorry, babe, you're on your own," he murmured, his eyes slowly closing. "I'm wasted . . ."

He lay sprawled on the bed, his bronzed skin in stark contrast to the whiteness of the sheets. His harshly modeled features and high cheekbones were cast into chiaroscuro in the moonlight, his long lashes—almost too beautiful for a man—lay in dark half-moons on his cheeks. Ceci stroked the black silk of his hair spread out on the pillow, feeling as though she'd known him a lifetime.

The mining companies on the Iron Range had gone to Europe to recruit cheap labor in the nineteenth century, concentrating their efforts on the poorest countries. So Slavs and Italians composed the majority of the population—handsome people with black hair and dark skin, and Zuber was no exception.

Although he was getting to be someone exceptional to her.

Hold on there, her voice of reason interposed. Hold on just one damned minute. Are we talking about Zuber?

She bitch-slapped her voice of reason because she was feeling really fine right now and didn't need logic or rational discourse within a mile of her thoughts.

He was damned gorgeous and damned good where it mattered.

She picked up her notebook and began writing.

CHAPTER 10

Lily smelled the bacon before she opened her eyes and it took her a moment to properly register where she was to be smelling bacon in the morning. And it was obviously morning, because the very, very brilliant, *too* brilliant light from the unshaded windows was hurting her eyes. She turned her head to evade the hideously searing light and came face-to-face with the man who had occupied her dreams last night.

"It's not a dream," he said, his mind-reading abilities in fine form, or perhaps her shock gave him a clue. He handed her a latte in one of the Lodge's large white cups. "Two brown sugars, I hope that's okay." And then he sat down on the edge of the bed and took a sip from his latte.

"You were in the kitchen last night," she said, her

gaze wary. She glanced down at her cup. "And you were at the Lodge this morning."

"Yes and no. They brought over the lattes."

"And?"

"What else would you like to know? And don't ask about Tammy, because we went over that last night ad nauseam."

"Tammy?"

"The black-haired bitch."

It all came flooding back, or more aptly, trickling back. "You stayed here last night?"

"In this bed, actually."

"With me?"

"Yeah. You shot me down on the ménage à trois. Just kidding," he quickly said at the look in her eye.

"You put something in my drink," she accused.

"I wasn't with you, if you recall. Maybe it was Mr. Dockers."

She groaned softly. In her snit with Billy, she'd given Charles-call-me-Chip her phone number. Now, it didn't seem like such a good idea.

"Having second thoughts about preppy men?"

"You can be very annoying."

"That's not what you said last night."

"You're obviously dying to tell me about last night, so tell me." She took a large gulp of coffee as though she might need it.

"There's nothing much to tell. While I was making you some coffee, you fell asleep with your head on the kitchen table. I carried you in here, put you to bed, and went to sleep."

"Sure you did."

He shrugged. "Not much point in having sex with a corpse."

"So it wasn't chivalry."

He grinned. "Some of it was. I could have wakened you if I wanted. Drink your latte and quit breaking my balls. I was a Boy Scout last night."

Her feelings were a chaotic mix of irritation at his presumption and the flagrantly libidinous cravings that always overtook her when he was in sight. "Don't you have to work?"

He shook his head. "Took the day off."

"Why?"

"I thought I'd spend it in bed with you. But you should eat first. There's some breakfast in the kitchen."

"What if I don't want to?"

"You should anyway," he said, as if he didn't know what she meant. "Breakfast is the most important meal of the day."

She looked at him squinty-eyed. "Does everyone always say yes to you?"

"No."

But the infinitesimal pause before he responded was answer enough. "I *could* be busy today," she said.

"Change your plans."

"Why should I do that?"

"Because we fit together *real* well, if you recall. And according to my mother, Myrtle Carlson has gone to visit her daughter in Biwabik so she won't hear you scream when you come."

Lily was instantly wet, as though he had only to promise her sex and she was ready. "How does your mother know that?" she asked in a voice that registered sexual desire in every suppressed syllable.

"They're both in the church choir."

She groaned softly. "I forgot how everyone knows everything about everyone in a small town."

Her orgasmic screams that night at the Lodge were a case in point, but he thought it might be counterproductive to mention it. "Look at the bright side," he said, rising from the bed. "We're alone out here today. Breakfast is ready in the kitchen and afterward"—he smiled—"we can do whatever you want."

It was difficult eating breakfast with the thought of doing whatever she wanted in the forefront of her thoughts. It was damned near impossible if she spent too much time recounting the inspired, really endearing whatever-you-want pleasures of their first night together. And it didn't help whatever moderate and judicious emotions she might still retain to be gazing up close and personal at darling Billy, God's gift to women. After a night of drinking, her senses were on high alert to everything sexual and the most beautifully sexual man she'd ever met was sitting across the table from her.

He'd changed sometime between the saloon last night and now, his blue striped camp shirt pressed and neat, his chino shorts without a wrinkle. She

wished she'd washed her robe, she thought, suddenly aware of a chocolate stain she'd intended to
swab with stain stick.

"You're not eating," he said. "Eat."

She folded some of the robe skirt over the stain.
"I ate a whole pint of ice cream last night and a
pastry and a candy bar."

He grinned. "You were missing me."

"Was not. Tell me about Tammy," she said,
wanting to make him squirm instead. "If we had a
conversation, I don't remember."

"Will you eat then? I don't want you wasting
away."

He was either incredibly sweet or incredibly
smooth, but at the moment she didn't care because
she didn't feel like fasting *or* eating raw vegetables
when she had a mushroom-and-bacon omelette on
her plate, a basket of blueberry muffins was scenting the air, and the strawberries in the bowl to her
left were arranged in a little mountain with
whipped cream on top. She reached for a muffin.

He leaned back in his chair and offered her an
easygoing smile. "I took Tammy home, said thanks
but no thanks, I have to get up early in the morning, and drove around for an hour or so, telling myself I wasn't coming over here. And then I came over
here and you proceeded to tell me you missed me."

"Did not," she said, not looking up from butter-
ing her muffin in case he could see her embarrassment.

"Yeah, you did. But then you also said all men

were scum, so I wasn't so sure about the signals I was getting. Although you did mention your orgasms that night at the Lodge were mind-blowing, so I thought that was probably a plus in my column."

She flushed red. "You're making this up."

"You wish. But just when I thought things were going my way, you passed out on the kitchen table and ruined all my plans." His smile broadened. "But I'm still hopeful."

"I should send you home," she said, although the words were slightly muffled by her mouthful of muffin.

He only smiled, picked up his latte cup and lounged back in his chair, looking immaculate—all fresh shirted and shorted—and apparently immune to hunger while she was eating everything in sight. "Aren't you eating?"

"We don't all sleep until ten." He waved toward some dirty dishes on the counter. "I ate hours ago and then raked your beach and took your canoe down from the boathouse wall. That's a nice old Grumman."

"It was my dad's," she said, taking note of the Lodge logo on the dishes on her counter. "You had the cook come here twice?"

"Gracie doesn't mind."

"How old is this Gracie?"

He looked entertained. "Thirty-one. Same age as you."

"It's none of my business, I'm sure," she said.

"True."

"You're very annoying speaking in that courteous, polite, butter-wouldn't-melt-in-your-mouth voice."

"You're just touchy because you're hungover," he said pleasantly.

She put down her fork. "What if I said we weren't going to have sex. Would that unruffle your calm?"

"I don't think you're going to say that."

"I could."

He worked hard at suppressing his grin. "Well, then I'd just have to suffer, I guess."

"Bloody right, you would."

"Or you would."

"You think I can't go without sex?"

He shrugged. "You're hungover. You need food, sex, a couple of Cokes with lots of ice, not necessarily in that order."

"And you're available."

"Unless you'd prefer Mr. Dockers. The Cokes are in the fridge, by the way."

"How do you know I don't like Pepsi?"

"Because you always drank Coke at the beach. And I've an excellent memory of you."

Her memories of him were more recent, but equally good—crystal clear in fact, which was why her libido was craving sex, not in general, but very specifically with him. "Damn," she said under her breath, thinking every woman he knew probably responded to him the same way.

"Try the strawberries. They're locally grown."

"So you can wait all day, Mr. Casual-try-the-strawberries?"

"Not really," he said, coming to his feet, his erection lifting the pleated front of his chino shorts.

She flushed, took a small breath, put down her fork and rose from her chair. "Thank you for breakfast."

"I'll bring the Cokes."

She nodded.

Apparently there was a limit to sexual restraint and she'd reached it. And whether she was one of hundreds in his female entourage didn't matter right now. Right now, she wanted to have sex.

He stepped over her robe as he followed her down the hall, and when he entered her bedroom, she was lying naked on her bed, looking like every man's dream with her legs spread wide and her arms open in welcome. "What took so long?" she said, wiggling her fingers like a fidgety child.

He set down the Cokes and stripped off his clothes while she watched him, restless and impatient, no longer caring about anything but consummation. His skin was bronzed, not from the sun, but everywhere, his lithe muscled body blatantly aphrodisiac, the heated look in his eyes sending a thrill through her senses. He'd discarded his shirt, his shorts, and when he slid his boxers down his legs and his erection sprang free, she felt out of control. Whimpering, she slid her feet upward, let her thighs fall open. "Please, please, please," she whispered.

As impatient as she, perhaps more so after waiting all night, he quickly lowered himself between her legs and then swore softly. He'd forgotten a condom.

"It doesn't matter," she whispered, lifting her hips to draw him in.

He took a deep breath, exhaled slowly. "Yeah, it does." Rolling back on his heels, he stretched over the side of the bed, picked up his shorts, pulled out a foil packet from his pocket, ripped it open, put on a condom and swung back between her legs. "I hope that didn't break your stride." His smile was warm on her mouth.

"Right now, I could damn near come without you," she whispered, running her palms down his spine.

"Hold on," he murmured, gliding in slowly, feeling her sleek flesh give way. "I'm comin' on in . . ."

She sighed, bliss beginning to color her world.

Ignoring preliminaries and foreplay in the interests of her neediness, he buried himself in her soft, welcoming warmth. Although his impatience matched hers after his long, frustrating night of waiting, he drove in deeper, swallowing her soft breathy cry, propelling her upward on the bed with the sheer force of his invasion. Heedless to all but carnal satisfaction, she melted around him, rose into his downward thrust, tempestuously met the sensational rhythm of his lower body, her impassioned senses peaking fast and furiously. . .

The phone rang, but neither noticed.

Serena's voice on the answering machine drifted in and out of their consciousness, wordless sounds, inaudible words, background resonance to the pounding in their ears, to the heated oscillation of their bodies, to the tropical heat wave of sensation too long delayed, intensified by morning-after sensibilities—carrying them in a rush tide toward orgasm. The message went on and on while the slippery flux and flow of their rocking bodies neared the combustible sublime. Lily whimpered once, twice, as the terrifyingly single-minded orgasmic force swelled inside her, and then she cried out, a long, keening, high-pitched scream that would have gained Myrtle Carlson's attention had she been home. Holding his breath against the convulsive frenzy, the tension in his arms swelling his biceps, he felt that first ejaculatory rush clear down to his toes, and for long, fierce, seemingly endless moments they shared the awesome, cataclysmic, mind-blowing glory.

As their last orgasmic ripples died away, Serena's voice finally infiltrated their consciousness.

". . . tea at my house this afternoon," she was saying. "You know my mom's teas." She giggled. "See you at three . . ."

Lily felt Billy's chuckle and opened her eyes marginally, blissful lethargy weighting her lashes.

"Your friend sure likes to talk."

"You didn't seem bothered."

He grinned. "I didn't notice you missing a beat."

"I've been waiting since last night."

"No kidding." He kissed her gently and then glanced at the clock. "And it's still early."

She drew her finger over the curve of his mouth and smiled. "How nice."

"Yeah, nice," he said, kissing her lightly before withdrawing. Although that wouldn't be his choice of words for this insatiable hard-on craving he had for her. "Towels?" he said a moment later and she pointed toward the bathroom.

She should get up, she thought, but it was easier to lie still and absorb the dreamy summer morning and think of the dreamy man who had just made love to her and was probably wading through the mess in her bathroom that she had planned on picking up before she went out last night. Shit. She came up on her elbows at the thought, but now that lust wasn't pouring endorphins into her bloodstream, her head didn't like the sudden movement and she lay back down, praying that Billy wasn't overly fond of Martha Stewart types.

"Eureka," he said, a moment later, standing in the doorway holding a hand towel that looked very small in his large hand.

"I don't have maid service like you," she said, recalling his immaculate cabin.

"I could send someone over."

"There's more towels in the hall linen closet. I went swimming yesterday," she said, feeling as though she had to explain when he was obviously unused to an empty towel shelf. "And then I took a shower before I went out and the shower curtain wasn't in the tub, I guess, so I had to throw towels on the floor to sop up—"

"I'm just offering some of the staff from the Lodge if you like. I wiped up the floor and threw the towels in the tub."

She should have suspected, when he always looked as if he'd stepped out of a page from *GQ*, that he was used to neat. His mother had probably ironed his jeans. Her mother only cleaned when company was coming over—correction—she marshaled the family to clean when someone was coming over. "Thanks, I'll think about it," she said, playing the odds that Billy would have forgotten her name in a week. And if she was going to live on a teacher's salary this year, she'd better get used to cleaning her own house.

"They could do your wash for you too," he said, stepping over her clothes on the floor.

"I couldn't decide what to wear last night."

"You looked great."

She mentally scrutinized his comment, but didn't discern censure or irony and he was smiling. He was also looking like some beautiful Greek god walking toward her, really unbelievably buff and hard, hard, *hard,* and she decided not to further dissect nuances of meaning in favor of simply enjoying the towering, well—view.

"It's really turning me on," she blurted out, "I mean—you, oh hell, you know what I mean." And then she turned ten shades of red because she hadn't intended to say what she was thinking. Although he didn't seem to mind. He was grinning.

"Well, that works out then," he said, moving toward her, his smile sportive now and sexy as hell, "because it's hard for a reason. And if you keep lying there with your legs spread, I'm not going to be leaving any time soon."

She didn't move and his smile broadened.

But he didn't seem to be in any hurry. He sat on the edge of the bed, picked up one of the Cokes he'd brought in from the kitchen, offered it to her, held it to her mouth as she half-rose to take a sip. "Done? Is that all?" he said a moment later and then drained the glass as she lay back down. Pouring some ice cubes into his mouth, he sucked on them for a second and then dropped them in his hand. "Don't move," he said.

A tiny frisson ran up her spine and she didn't.

He slipped the ice cubes into her pulsing cleft, pushed them upward while she shivered from lust not cold. "You okay?" he murmured, leaning over to lick a slow path down her belly.

She felt him outside and in—or the prelude of him inside, the coolness melting, oozing downward, and she decided he'd have to read her mind if he wanted an answer.

Apparently, he did that, because he moved her so he could get closer and lick away the melting ice.

The pressure of his tongue slid up her labia— first one side, then the other—and then glided down her slit. She moaned, lifted her hips, instantly incited, impatient. He understood what she wanted, and parting her labia with his fingers, he delicately licked the throbbing nub of her clitoris. He took his time, sliding his tongue around and around, slowly, slowly, up and down even more slowly until all sensation was hotly focused on one tiny location and her body was aching for release. "Ready?" he said into the liquid warmth of her body, not really expecting an answer when she was panting like that. His lips closed over her hard clit a second later and while she sobbed and cried and quivered in ecstasy, he gently sucked her orgasm into his mouth.

She couldn't move afterward.

She couldn't talk.

Eyes shut, her heart pounding, she lay there dissolving in happiness for what seemed eons. When she was finally able to breathe, when her eyes seemed capable of opening without a derrick, she lifted her lashes and saw him sitting between her legs, watching her.

He smiled. "You're cute."

Childish cute? Sexy cute? Cute like Cabbage Patch Kids or like Kate Moss? You wish, she instantly rebuked herself on the latter, and throwing caution to the wind in her mood of sublime bliss, said, "How?"

"I don't know. Like easy." At her frown, he corrected himself. "Easy to please, I mean."

Thinking that had to be a positive for a guy, she

smiled at him. "You're just good." And it wasn't flattery. She meant it with every satisfied fiber of her being. In the roseate afterglow of the most incredible, outstanding orgasm, she was even able to overlook the probable reasons for his expertise.

"I'm just motivated," he said, running his palms lightly up her legs, gripping her thighs, pulling her closer. "Really motivated," he whispered, stroking the blond curls on her mons.

She knew what he meant. His erection was twitching against his stomach, as if it couldn't wait to get inside, and she could feel herself getting motivated too. Reaching up, she pulled on his arms and he bent to kiss her.

"I don't want kisses," she whispered.

His smile brushed her mouth. "What do you want?"

"This," she said, touching the head of his erection.

It took him a second to answer; she could feel his penis swell.

"Where do you want it?" he said, a raspy undertone to his voice, brushing her hand away, sitting up and reaching for a condom.

Gripping his penis seconds later, she slid up on the bed, pulling him with her. "I want this here," she said, spreading her thighs, placing the tip in the slit of her labia. "And I don't want to wait."

She didn't have to, not that time or any of the other times that day. They were both on the same freight train.

And while he said, "My turn this time," he didn't mean it, or if he did, he was one unselfish guy because she managed to come several times more. He really, really, *really* took his time, until she was beginning to wonder if he had read those books on Tantric sex. When he finally did come again, and a considerable time after that when she could stop panting long enough to speak, she asked him. "Tantra who?" he responded.

Not that it mattered when he seemed to understand the ancient sexual practice in some completely natural male way of his own. And if he hadn't been smiling at her with his sexiest-man-in-the-world smile, she might have explained it wasn't a who but a what. As it was, her body was responding to that smile in a completely predictable way or at least a completely predictable way since she'd met Billy Bianchich.

"More Coke?" He lifted the glass from the bedside table and offered it to her.

"I'd rather have more cock."

"Cute." His dark brows flickered. "How about both?"

"Where?"

He grinned. "You're on a roll."

"Try hungover and ravenous."

He tipped his head. "Told you."

"So?"

"Open your mouth," he said, very, very softly.

A little Coke, a little cock, turned into a delicious mantra as well as several fevered positions that inspired a blur of wild orgasms and strongly encouraged the belief in an earthly paradise.

But as it neared three, Lily said, "I have to go," for the tenth time since two when she really should have started getting ready.

"Don't go." He traced a fingertip lightly down her cleft. "Tell Serena and her mother you're busy."

He'd slipped his finger inside her and started doing his magic, but Lily took a deep breath, thought maybe two dozen orgasms were enough for one day, knew that Buffy Howard's invitations were more like royal commands, and said, "I can't."

"You don't want to, you mean." He rolled away, looking sullen.

"I would if I could. You know Buffy Howard. She'll send her yard man, slash, chauffeur, slash, enforcer, Vinnie, here to drag me out if I don't show."

He snorted. "Vinnie's a hundred years old."

"But hard to say no to."

"*I'll* tell him no."

He looked as if he wanted to, but it wouldn't have been fair, because Vinnie was probably a hundred and ten if he was a day. "Wait here if you want. It shouldn't take long," she lied, knowing how Buffy's teas weren't really teas, but the finest of Veuve Cliquot Grande Dame moments that eluded your memory the next day.

He gave her a flinty look.

"I'm sorry."

"Right."

Something snapped when he said *right* like that.

Something that had to do with Brock, his pursed lips and their hotly contested property settlement—the one where he wanted everything. It was a male thing about winning and control, her lawyers had told her, although at the time, like now, she didn't give a shit about male-driven psychological impulses. After their bloody divorce settlement, she'd promised herself to stay clear of controlling men. And even hours of the world's best sex wasn't going to change her mind. "I didn't invite you over," she said, sitting up. "You showed up on your own."

"I didn't hear you complaining when you were coming every thirty seconds."

"The sex was great. Thanks." She rose from the bed and walked toward the bathroom. "You know the way out."

"Fuck you."

"I'll take a rain check," she said, oversweet like someone named Betty-Sue who lived south of the Mason-Dixon line might. Then she walked into the bathroom, shut the door, swore when she saw the orderly pile of towels in the tub, wrathfully tossed them out, and turned on the shower full blast.

She didn't hear him leave, but then she wasn't really listening.

CHAPTER 11

Buffy Howard greeted Lily and Ceci from her high-backed Jacobean tapestry-covered armchair that was set out under the old maple tree in the backyard. "You know everyone, darlings." She called everyone "darling," except her husband, whom she called "My Georgie Pie." That always sounded strange because Mr. Howard was tall, thin, gray-haired, almost completely silent, and the farthest thing from a Georgie Pie anyone could imagine. But then one preferred not thinking of parents having sex. No doubt there was some complex with a Greek name that explained it all.

Buffy waved them into seats, her huge diamonds twinkling on her fingers. "Come and tell us what you've been doing."

Ceci and Lily looked at each other, schooled

their faces into bland masks, said, "Not much," and sat.

A large Persian-style rug had been spread on the grass. A table covered in a richly embroidered white linen cloth, with enough crystal and silver to float the budget of a small third-world country, graced its surface. Several chairs surrounded the table and a number of familiar ladies smiled at them.

Buffy's maid-of-all-work, Stella, poured them champagne when they sat down, then retired to her chair in a nearby rose arbor that wasn't blooming yet because spring was always late in Ely, fall was early, and summer was jammed into the few brief, but idyllic, weeks in between.

"Serena tells me you're home all of next year, Lily," Buffy said. "Won't that be nice."

"I'm really looking forward to it," Lily said, careful to be enthusiastic with the dean's wife sitting across from her.

"Jeffrey is looking forward to working with you," Selma Wells said, her Boston accent as perfect as it was the day she first came to Ely thirty years ago.

The initial conversation consisted of the usual catching-up politesse, with all the appropriate welcomes and general information exchanged. Ceci updated the ladies on her design business in Sausalito and the state of their parents' respective vacations was discussed: Lily's folks, retired from teaching as of last year, were working in Tennessee this summer for Habitat for Humanity; Ceci's parents had put their insurance business in the hands of a nephew for the summer and were exploring their roots in Sicily and Milan.

Aunt Bernie was the first to broach the subject of Lily's divorce. She'd been leaning forward in her chair for the last ten minutes, waiting for a break in the conversation. "Your mother told me before she left that you had to put up a real fight for your cabin in the divorce. My word! Your husband must have been greedy! He never even spent any time here!"

Greedy was a relatively kind description of Brock, Lily thought, her own assessment composed of less polite terms. "He didn't actually want it, but negotiations go that way. You pretend you want something so you have more leverage on the property you really want." Lily smiled ruefully. "One learns."

"But he's out of her life and Lily is really glad," Ceci interposed. "Although I could have saved her the trouble of a divorce if she'd asked me my advice before she got married."

"Speaking of marriage, darling," Buffy said brightly, "have you a special beau?" A good marriage, i.e., a wealthy one, was Buffy's Holy Grail.

Her recent hours in bed with Zuber were definitely special, Ceci thought, but Buffy probably didn't mean that. "I'm not sure I'll get married." She shrugged. "Independence appeals to me."

"You see, Mother, I'm not the only one who feels that way. Thank you, Ceci," Serena cooed, casting her mother an I-told-you-so look, because even though she might be in *love* with Frankie, she had no intention of marrying a man who lived in Ely—two hundred fifty miles from decent shopping.

"The world is changing, Buffy. All the girls of our generation were married by the time they were twenty," Georgina Marcetti said. "Of course, they didn't all stay married."

A variety of nods and murmurs indicating approval and disapproval went around the table.

"You just have to find the right person," Aunt Bernie declared smugly. In her case, her husband, the mayor, mayored during the week and fished or hunted every weekend with his buddies, leaving Bernie free to entertain herself with her friends which was as near to a perfect marriage as man could devise.

"I agree," Buffy said, touching the large diamond studs in her ears, evidence of her own good judgment. "Someday, Serena, you'll find that special someone. There's someone for everyone . . ."

"Isn't that a line from a song?" Ceci said lightly.

"No, it's a tiresome old platitude." Serena was scowling.

"Mock all you want, darlings," Buffy said, admiring the sun through her champagne glass. "But you might find yourself living in Ely someday after all." The Southern belle descended from a long line of Maryland senators had met her Georgie Pie when he'd come down from Yale to visit her brother, so she knew of what she spoke.

"I won't," Serena retorted mutinously.

"You can't fault it for summer vacations," Ceci observed, stepping in to ward off an argument, knowing very well *she'd* never be living here. "And you *have* been having fun since you came home, Serena."

The familiar dreamy look came over Serena's face—the one that always appeared when Frankie was mentioned. "It *has* been nice," Serena agreed, looking off into the distance like the woman sipping on Hazelnut Vanilla Creme coffee in a Taster's Choice commercial.

Buffy signaled for more champagne to be poured; she knew how to mitigate controversy. And before long, the gossip had moved on to the fisticuffs at the last Eastern Star meeting.

Everything was pretty fuzzy when Lily and Ceci walked home several hours later, the champagne tea having brought back a flood of memories. Buffy had first let them drink champagne on their sixteenth birthdays—but only a token half-glass. As they grew older, their portions increased, and Buffy's tea parties were always a pleasant occasion between generations. Listening and learning at their mothers' gossipy knees as it were.

Ceci had already heard of Lily's ill-fated leave-taking of Billy, so she was careful not to ask any prying questions on the way home.

When they reached Ceci's driveway, Lily could see Zuber's Range Rover parked next to the cabin on the hill. "He didn't mind waiting, I see," she said.

"His schedule's tight this summer so he's taking advantage of his cancellation. He has to leave again in a few days."

"You never talked about him before. Did things change this summer?"

Ceci shrugged. "I don't know. I'm just along for the ride. And so is he. Don't take Billy's tantrum too seriously. He probably doesn't know what's going on in his head either." It just came out, but since it had, she added, "Billy doesn't take any woman to his place at the Lodge though. Just thought you should know."

"He's too temperamental. But thanks. If I want another prima donna in my life, I'll buy a Ballerina Barbie. Or I could always choose to be celibate. It's becoming fashionable."

"Sure. I can see that happening. About the time I join an order of monks in Nepal."

Lily laughed. "Celibacy should be easy enough tonight anyway. I came about a thousand times today. That should hold me till tomorrow." She waved. "Call me when Nick leaves."

CHAPTER **12**

Serena was going out with Frankie tonight, Ceci was in bed with Zuber, and Lily was going to see if her cable still worked. It did and she watched *The Naked Chef, Hardball,* and two episodes of *Arliss* before her hunger pangs drove her out of the house. She really should go to the grocery store, but it was easier to eat out tonight. Tomorrow, she'd buy some food.

It was late; the only restaurant open was the steak house and she really felt like having doughnuts. But doughnuts were only one food group, so to balance it off, she stopped at Zups deli and picked up a porchetta sandwich. To still her conscience, she also bought a tray of crudités with dill dip and a skim milk. Then she drove to Shagawa Beach, which used to be home to her in the summer, parked her car, took her bagged supper, walked over the two footbridges to the second island, and sat down on a rock to eat and watch the sun set. It was still light at ten o'clock this time of year.

She'd eaten the four doughnuts with assorted frostings, half the sandwich, one broccoli spear, and all her milk—a necessary sop to the four-food-groups fairy. And now she wished she had a Cosmopolitan in her hand while she admired the glorious sunset.

"I thought that was your car."

"Go away." She didn't turn around, but her pulse spiked.

"This is public property," Billy said, sitting on the rock beside her.

"Apparently." She started to bag up the remains of her supper.

"You're not going to eat that?"

She looked at him for a moment as if he were crazy.

"I've been driving around. I forgot to eat."

She handed him the bag and watched him devour her half-sandwich and all the crudités including the cauliflower ones, then lick the bottom of the dill dip container.

"What?" He gave her a blank stare.

"Nothing."

He rolled up the bag and squashed it between two rocks. "I seem to be chasing after you a lot." His voice was flat, mild even.

"Feel free not to."

"I wish I could feel free not to." He picked up a flat rock and skipped it about two dozen times.

He did everything well, didn't he, she thought, disgruntled with his numerous skills—his sexual ones foremost in her thoughts—and the various females who were the recipients of that skill pissing her off mightily. When she should know better.

"Wanna go show?"

Her head snapped around and she saw his grin.

"We talk different up here."

"I know, but there's still asses everywhere."

"Would it help if I got down on my knees?" At her shocked look, he quickly said, "To apologize."

She blew out a breath. "Jeez, that was scary."

"For us both," he said with a smile. "And I do apologize. I drove to the Queen City of Virginia twice since I left you, then over to Aurora and back. I don't even know why I came down here, but I'm glad I did. And if you want to see a movie, I'd like to take you. We could go on a date. We could go out for Cokes and fries after."

"Or we could have Cokes at my house," she said, thinking one had to be practical when a man like Billy Bianchich was apologizing and looking real, real sexy only inches away. Besides, the Cokes they had this morning were one of the great memories of her life.

"Better yet," he said, getting down on one knee and giving her a first-class, grade-A, hangdog look. "Am I forgiven then?"

"It depends." There was no point in looking too easy.

"On?"

"How good you are to me."

He placed his hands on her knees and gently eased her legs open. "I promise to be good. I like your skirt. Practical," he said, not referring to function or design, but to convenience. Slipping his hands under the flowered muslin, he brushed his palms up her thighs, touched the silk crotch of her panties with his thumbs, and exerted the faintest pressure.

She softly moaned.

He glanced around, taking in the few remaining people on the beach two islands away, the fishermen in a distant boat—everything else solitude. Coming to his feet, he pulled her up and led her under the low branches of a Douglas fir that had been planted during CCC days. The ground was soft with pine needles, but he took off his shirt anyway and spread it over the dry, scented needles.

"Someone might see."

"Everyone's gone." He sat down and drew her onto his lap, exhaling softly as she acquiesced, having thought of nothing but making love to her the entire time he was scorching up the highway. Thinking only of this while the music was blasting—of holding her, touching her, wanting it all to make sense when it didn't. Wanting more not to give a damn.

He kissed her gently, her mouth opened under his, and he was happy.

Happiness must have been contagious, because Lily inhaled it with his kiss.

He rolled onto his back, holding her close, still kissing her, and she lay atop him thinking how incredibly good he tasted, his bared chest warm through the cotton of her blouse, the beat of his heart faint against hers. The sunset seemed more golden, the air purer, life sweeter.

Hallmark sentimentality, but she didn't care. She didn't care that she might be stupid to let Billy Bianchich flip-flop her world from misery to ecstasy in five minutes flat. Ummm . . . although there were definite rewards. She moved her hips back and forth over his erection. He *had* missed her. And she was doing way too much thinking when there were better things to do.

He eased her skirt up over her hips a moment later, slipped her panties off with finesse. No fumbling with Billy—a pleasant and not so pleasant thought. But then he rolled over, covered her body with his, and where he'd acquired his expertise seemed less important than the fact that he was lying above her, his dark eyes so beautiful she would have melted at the sight if she wasn't already a puddle of longing.

"I thought of you every second today." His voice was velvety, low. "Of holding you like this . . . making love to you."

"I thought about killing you today . . . sort of— once or twice." She smiled. "But not lately."

"So kill me." Opening his zipper, he moved between her thighs.

"As if I could."

"You nearly have, babe. I'm on the ropes." He kicked off his shorts and boxers.

How incredibly sweet even if he was lying. "Could we talk later?" The last thing she wanted to do right now was cause him bodily harm unless fucking him to death counted.

He laughed. "In a hurry for something?" But he was ripping open a condom pack as he spoke.

"Oh, yeah."

"Me too."

"So?" She meant it to sound nonchalant, like a woman having a summer fling might sound, but he slid inside her just then and her voice did a little trill up the scale.

He nodded toward the lake and put a finger to his mouth.

She saw the boat and fishermen no more than twenty feet away. "I'll be quiet," she whispered.

He knew she was going to scream even if she didn't know it, but this wasn't the time to argue. He swung his hips back for the next downstroke.

"My God!" Her hissed exclamation stopped him mid-swing. She was staring at the boat. "That's Brad Mattson."

He almost jerked out but he wasn't a masochist.

He frowned though. Lily and Brad had been an item in high school. "I don't wanna hear this."

"Sorry. It's just—I haven't seen him since high school."

"If you're going to talk about some other guy, I'm outta here." Where the hell had that come from?

Her gaze swung back to him. "You're jealous."

"Fuck no." He couldn't be. He refused to be. Even though he knew something about Lily was different.

"I never slept with him."

"I don't care."

Her eyes held a hint of amusement. "It seemed like you might."

"Well, I don't, and nobody's jealous, okay?"

"Does that mean you're going to stay?" she purred, moving her hips slightly.

He shot a quick glance at Brad Mattson. "I guess."

"You guess?" Little icicles dripped from her words.

He kissed her then, because he wasn't going anywhere right now—except deeper.

She twisted her mouth away, but he took her chin between his thumb and forefinger and forced her face around. "I'm going to fuck you, right here, right now. And if you don't want your old boyfriend to watch, I'd suggest you keep it down."

She began to sputter, but he covered her mouth

with his, silenced her protest, and did what he said he was going to do—with authority and his usual gifted talents. Before long, Lily forgot to be mad. In fact, she soon forgot everything but fevered sensation because she was filled with cock and Billy was telling her if she was real good, he'd stay right there, hard and long and deep, until she was done coming.

What was a girl to do?

It was dark by the time they were finished.

The fishing boat was gone.

Billy was lying beside Lily, thinking life couldn't get any better. "I might be a little jealous," he said.

Lily was half-asleep, her body still warm from making love. "You don't have to be polite," she said mildly, lifting her lashes enough to see him. "I'm more than content."

He drew in a breath, debating his reaction to such casualness. But wisdom prevailed, or force of habit. Casual was good. "Fine," he said. "I'm glad. We're both content."

CHAPTER **13**

"Would you ever live in the city?" Serena asked, as she and Frankie lay in his hammock, the sky above the lake bright with stars.

"Hell, no." She went silent and he realized he'd given the wrong answer. "How big a city?" he hedged.

She snuggled closer and gave a little sigh. "I don't know. Bigger than Ely."

"Don't you like it here?"

"Everyone knows everyone."

"You don't like that?"

"Not really."

"Sometimes it's nice. When you need help or a ride somewhere or a new roof on your house."

"Frankie," she said with a touch of exasperation. "You make it sound like the frontier."

"It *is* the end of the road. Canada's on the other side of the lake."

"There's so much more to do in the big city. Clubs and dancing, shopping . . ." Her voice trailed off. "I suppose men don't care about that."

"Not the shopping anyway. The cities aren't so far if you're looking for that stuff." He didn't say he'd been offered a job as the governor's bodyguard, but he'd turned it down. If he lived in the capital, he couldn't piss off his dock in the morning and life would be a lot more complicated.

A small silence fell.

"Do we have to talk about this now?" he asked, reverting to normal male behavior, putting off controversy.

Serena sighed. "No."

"I'd like to make you happy."

"I know."

"Do you want to go dancing?"

"You have to be at work at seven." Serena wouldn't have even understood the concept of empathy before. It was a startling measure of her affection.

"We could go dancing tomorrow night."

She smiled into the starlit sky. "I'd like that. You haven't seen my new red dress."

"Is it hard to get off?"

"Just one zipper."

"Then I'm going to love it. You've got a date."

Frankie tucked the covers over Serena's shoulders that morning when he left for work and gently kissed her cheek. She stirred in her sleep and smiled and he knew what it felt like to be on top of the world. Not that he was unrealistic about Serena Howard and her life beyond the circumscribed boundaries of Ely. But he was enjoying himself while he could. It was the only sensible thing to do.

She didn't like Ely.

And he wasn't a big-city boy.

CHAPTER **14**

The men met for breakfast that morning, as they often did. Billy had left Lily with a kiss and a promise to be back for supper. She was going to cook, she said—scary thought after she'd asked him if he liked sushi—and he had to work at the store. Zuber was on a mission for food and was bringing Ceci back a take-out breakfast, because he had one day left of his unplanned vacation and they were cocooning until he headed uplake again.

Frankie was seated in their corner booth at Vertins, not necessarily planning on company, but not surprised when his friends appeared. The men had been eating breakfast together in the summer for a long time.

Frankie nodded as his friends walked up. "Howzit goin'?"

"Not bad," Billy said, sitting down and giving Jolene who owned the place a wave and a smile.

Not bad was about as good as it got in the language of the Range. Frankie and Zuber grinned at each other.

Zuber greeted Jolene, who had come up with the coffeepot, pointed at his cup, and turned to Billy. "Done driving around then?" Billy had called Zuber from Aurora about five yesterday and asked him if he wanted to drink at the Legion.

"Yeah."

"Good summer so far," Zuber said.

"Can't complain," Billy said, smiling.

"Fucking A," Frankie said.

And that was about as close as they were going to get to talking about their feelings.

Serena came over to Lily's after she woke up, and they ate Oreos and milk for breakfast. Oreos lasted on the shelf even over the winter and Lily had called the local dairy for delivery when she'd arrived so the milk was fresh.

"Order their apple pie ice cream," Serena said, taking the second to the last cookie in the bag. "It's the best. Like Frankie."

"You really like him, don't you." It was the understatement of the century after Serena's descriptions of his various awesome wonders in the course of their Oreo breakfast. Not that Lily needed to know that Frankie's skin was so dark down there,

Serena had taken to calling his you-know-what "Black Beauty."

"I've been wasting my time on old men."

"Well, that's good to know," Lily said, instead of, "It's about time," which was what she was thinking.

"But I don't think Frankie and I have much of a future."

"Why don't we just consider this summer our little fling," Lily said. "We'll enjoy ourselves without thinking about tomorrow . . . or hell—about anything at all, beyond the—"

"*Great* sex."

"Great, *great* sex," Lily said, smiling, a host of blissful making-love scenarios flashing through her mind.

"Like Ceci does."

"Exactly, and she seems pretty happy."

"I wish Mother would stop talking about marriage, though. It's so annoying. Daddy never does. He says, 'Just remember, we're always here for you, Baby. You go out and enjoy yourself.' " She smiled. "He still calls me 'Baby.' "

"My dad does too, although it's mostly when he's introducing me to his friends at the golf course." Her father had been the golf coach at the high school. "So, we'll just live in the moment. I'm glad so many of my moments of late have been orgasmic."

Serena giggled. "How many times have you come in a row? I didn't even know it could happen."

Lily smiled. "I haven't paid attention. I'll count tonight."

Serena eventually went home, Lily went to the grocery store and intended to spend the rest of the afternoon cooking. But once she put the groceries away and ate her deli take-out, she decided to lie down for a short little nap before she started cooking. She hadn't slept much last night, not that she was complaining.

When Billy returned at six, he found a hideous-looking fish with two eyes on one side of its head thawing in the sink and Lily sleeping. He covered up the fish with a newspaper so he wouldn't have to look at it, opened the refrigerator hoping to find a beer, didn't, and ordered some brought up from the Lodge. While he was waiting, he took a quick shower. The beer was on the kitchen table when he came out of the bathroom. He took the rest of the paper out on the deck with his beer, sat down on the red-painted Adirondack chair, called a Vermillion chair in Boundary Waters country, and began to read.

He'd made a dozen house calls today, catching up after his day off yesterday. He'd repaired two water heaters, cleaned a furnace, put up a dozen new screens, helped one old lady plant her garden with the tools he'd brought out from the store, got two lawn mowers going again, and in general spread goodwill for Ace Hardware. He'd been doing this handyman stuff since he was fourteen, in between his hockey practice. It was relaxing because it was mindless, no-pressure work. He wasn't racing after some record number of goals for the year or seriously working out so he wouldn't break any bones or rip any tendons for another season; he wasn't wondering if some young Turk was going to try and take him on like some of them did, nor was he sitting at a press conference saying all the right things about team spirit and the great coach, about playing for the fun of it—although that was true. Once it stopped being fun though, he'd quit with no regrets.

He'd never been injured—knock on wood—which he did on the red-painted arm of the chair . . . and then did once more for good measure. He really liked the game; it was his passion and pleasure—not to mention the serious money he could make doing something he liked. And speaking of something he liked, he glanced at his watch.

He'd give Lily another twenty minutes to sleep.

They were bringing up dinner from the Lodge at seven.

CHAPTER 15

Lily woke up to a warm kiss and an icy cold Cosmopolitan made just the way she liked it, with extra cranberry juice and ice chips.

"I've died and gone to heaven," she purred, taking a sip as Billy held it to her mouth.

"Heaven comes later, babe," Billy said with a grin, standing with the glass in his hand. "Right now our dinner is getting cold and I haven't eaten since breakfast." The four burgers he ate in the truck didn't count.

"After watching you last night at Shagawa Beach, I have no wish to get between you and your supper. Throw me my robe."

"Not a chance."

"I don't suppose you'll see anything you haven't

seen before," Lily said, throwing the covers back and rising from the bed, nude.

He whistled. "Now that's what a man wants to see after a hard day's work." He set down the glass. "Maybe supper can wait after all." Gently cupping her breasts, he bent his head. "Ummm . . . just the way I like them—warm from bed."

The tip of his tongue grazed one nipple, the crest went instantly taut, and a frisson of pleasure streaked downward. As if she had an addiction to his touch, the familiar, greedy ache began to throb between her legs and she reached for the button at the waistband of his jeans.

He swung his hips back so her hand slid away. "Not so fast," he whispered, his breath warm on her breast. "I've barely had a taste."

"Maybe I don't want to wait." A poutiness underscored her words.

"Maybe you have to."

His mouth closed hard over her nipple and she forgot what she was about to say. Her breath caught in her throat as pleasure spiked through her body. Her fingers of their own accord slid through his hair and she hung on for dear life while he sucked, licked, tugged at her nipples—first one then the other, then back to the first in a leisurely, succulent tasting . . . as though he had all the time in the world. As though she wasn't holding her legs together against the riveting sensation, as though she wasn't whimpering for surcease.

He seemed not to notice; he lifted her breasts

higher, forcing her on her toes, biting her nipples in little nibbling bites that resonated through every heated cell in her body.

Finally, he released her, lifted his head and gave her a lazy smile. "Do you want something?" he drawled, as though he'd not been withholding sex when she desperately needed it.

"I'm going to kill you," she panted.

He reached for the zipper on his jeans, slow-motion, teasing. "Before or after?"

"During," she murmured, shoving his hands aside, unzipping his jeans herself, fast, dead-serious fast.

He smiled, but he didn't pull away this time, and when she fell back onto the bed, he followed her down and slid inside her, hard and long, smooth as silk. Her orgasm began before he was fully submerged, her whimpering sigh curling around his ears, her eagerness always a delight. And while he had more control, he understood eagerness—because he wanted her every minute of the day.

He didn't want to think too hard about the novelty of his feelings. Not now. Not when he was feeling this effing good.

Eventually, though, the delicious smells from the kitchen wafted their way into the bedroom, and the meagerness of Lily's Oreo breakfast and her deli snack lunch made Gracie's supper impossible to ignore. They were both lying on their backs, breathing hard, the remnants of a recent climax still strumming through their bodies. Drawing in a deep breath that tasted faintly of fresh bread, Lily turned her head on the pillow and looked at Billy. "Would you be offended," she said, "if—"

"Not if you aren't."

He definitely could read minds. She smiled. "You're so understanding about . . . well—everything."

He grinned. "I think we're both—"

"On the same page?"

"That'll do."

"No. What were you going to say?"

"I was going to say *obsessed*. See, yours was better."

"Do you mind being obsessed?"

All his perfect white teeth, maintained by Dr. Raab, the local dentist turned gourmet restaurateur, suddenly showed. "Hell, no."

"Good."

It was a lot better than good, but he only nodded and smiled. Good would do for now.

Lily pulled on a pair of shorts and a T-shirt for dining and Billy just put his jeans back on. Which did wonders for her view across the table.

"Are you happy?" she asked, after her second serving of shrimp fettuccine, knowing she shouldn't ask personal questions after knowing a man for such a short time, but feeling so blissfully content, she didn't care.

Billy didn't care either, a rare phenomenon if he'd taken note—which he didn't because his view across the table was incredible, his steak had been done just the way he liked it, and he really was happy. "Yes," he said. "Yes, I am," he elaborated.

His dazzling smile was sheer perfection, she thought. "I've decided to live in the moment," Lily said. "Like Zen."

"Do you study Zen?"

"Not really. I know a few principles and phrases. You're supposed to feel the bottom of your feet when you walk, you know."

He looked perplexed for a moment and then said, "Fine. Great. There's no one I'd rather live in the moment with, Miss Lily, sitting there all beautiful in your shirt with a picture of Miss Piggy on the front. Damned if *she* doesn't even look good."

"How much of that wine have you drunk?"

"All of it. You had the Cosmopolitans. I had the syrah."

She looked at the oversized cocktail shaker, noticed it was empty, and decided not to complain about his liquor consumption.

"Good idea," he said with a grin. "The pot and glass houses and all that. If you're done eating, I'll take you for a canoe ride."

She felt as though some Abou Ben Adhem had written a menu for happiness in a great book in the sky and Billy was reading from it. "Love to," she said. "Front or back?"

"Don't say that after a bottle of syrah."

"Fuck you."

"Don't say that either." He grinned. "I'll steer, 'cause I'm a man and you're a woman and we're on the Range and men steer canoes."

"I know how."

"I figured, but give me a break. Someone at the Lodge might see us and I'll never hear the end of it."

It wasn't as though women's lib hadn't reached the Iron Range. It just hadn't reached the Range when it came to paddling canoes.

The loons were calling across the lake, fishermen were coming back from their day's fishing, smoke from outdoor grills were curling up into the sky, the docks at the Lodge were busy with guides unpacking the supplies from their day trips, and Billy waved to everyone on shore and in boats who called out to him. Apparently, he was recognizable even at a distance. Lily felt a warm glow at the degree of affection accorded him, at the easygoing way he accepted it. After her ex-husband's gigantic ego that needed constant feeding, Billy's lack of vanity was refreshing.

He asked her if she wanted to stop at the Lodge bar.

"Have you noticed my coordination paddling?" she said.

"I thought all girls paddled that way."

She whipped water at him with her paddle and that only added to his already considerable allure, because now his nude torso was glistening wet. But he took over paddling then and she didn't demur. It was much nicer to just bask in the setting sun and her Cosmopolitan glow.

Billy took them on a tour of the southern half of the lake and then pulled up to Lily's dock as twilight fell. He slipped his arm around her waist as they walked up from the shore to the cabin and kissed her here and there.

Surely this was very close to Zen heaven.

They cleaned up the kitchen together, putting away the remains of their dinner, washing the dishes. Billy washed, she dried—someday she'd get a dishwasher, she'd always thought, but after the coziness of their shared task, now she wasn't so sure.

When they were done, he asked her if she wanted to watch TV.

"Do you?" He was beautiful beyond words, wearing only jeans, barefoot, his tanned sculpted body better than any Calvin Klein ad.

"Not really. I was being polite."

She must have sighed in relief because he laughed, and then said, "I'm sorry. You looked so cute, like you almost missed out on your Almond Joy."

"How did you know?"

"About the sex or the Almond Joy?"

"I know how you know about the sex and I don't want to talk about it."

"I saw the Almond Joy wrapper that night I came over."

"Good answer."

He grinned. "Thank you. Now could I interest you in a view of the lake from your bedroom?"

Much later that night, Billy muttered, "What the hell are you doing?"

"Nothing."

"You bloody well better not be counting."

"Serena wanted to know."

"I don't give a damn if the queen of England wants to know. You're freaking me out."

"Will it affect your—er . . . I mean—"

"Damn right it will."

Altruism lost out to selfish pleasure.

Lily stopped counting.

And Billy got his groove back.

CHAPTER 16

The following week, Billy began getting ready for his annual hockey camp—a day camp he sponsored for the local kids. Zuber was out of town in the Boundary Waters and Frankie had to be in court in Virginia for a trial that involved his department.

Serena agreed to visit a potter for her mother and select some new items for the store. Buffy trusted her daughter's taste. If nothing else, Serena knew quality; she'd been a serious shopper for years.

Ceci was working on her poetry, eschewing the nightlife in Ely for the first time in her life and waiting for Zuber's return.

Lily had begun a new garden at the lake and was busy planting a variety of perennials she hoped to winter over with a heavy mulch and much prayer.

"Lots of luck," Billy had said, looking at her

colorful display, few of which he recognized. "Those don't actually grow in Ely, do they?"

"They're going to this year," Lily had said firmly.

"An experiment?"

"No."

"You *are* a dreamer."

And maybe she was, because Billy was still around after a week.

But into every world, some rain must fall.

It started raining—figuratively speaking—on Tuesday.

Billy had asked Lily to pick him up at the hockey arena after the first day of camp. "I'll show you around, once all the munchkins leave," he'd said. "And then I'll take you to dinner—you pick a spot." His invitation was predicated more on survival than chivalry. Lily had cooked for them the previous night. She called it lasagna, but it didn't look, smell, or taste like lasagna. Swallowing down one serving had required a full bottle of Chianti.

The parking lot at the arena was mostly empty when Lily arrived. She'd planted, watered, and mulched thirty semirare woodland orchids in the birches east of her cabin and she was pleased. The dappled sunlight should be perfect, they would be away from the brunt of the winter storms, and the soil was the moist leaf compost they preferred. She crossed her fingers as she exited the car, wishing for good luck on their survival.

The arena was quiet when she walked inside. Nothing had changed much in the years she'd been gone. The signs on the walls were the same, the display cases with trophies were still in place, the snack bar had a new window with an espresso machine, but everything else was unaltered.

She moved toward the door that opened onto the rink and bleachers.

Pulling the door open and stepping inside, she scanned the area, looking for Billy. Only a few lights were on and it took her eyes a moment to become accustomed to the dimness. She heard the voices before she saw them.

Billy was standing very close to a small, red-haired woman or she was standing close to him. And they were laughing.

It shouldn't matter.

She was a fool to let it matter.

Billy wasn't hers. Not by the farthest stretch.

But it took her a few moments and some stern internal dialogue to bring her pulse rate back to near normal. And then another small interval before she was able to move forward.

He heard her walking down the cement stairs and turned and waved.

Lily waved back, casually, she hoped. She couldn't be certain with an ungovernable jealousy burning through her brain. When she reached where they stood on the verge of the ice, the woman looked at her as if she was gauging her right to be there.

"Lily, come meet Heather. We knew each other in high school."

"We were *good* friends in high school," Heather said, her soft tone making it clear how good their friendship was.

Billy seemed not to notice. "Lily's teaching at the community college next year," he said. "Botany."

"Really."

Heather made it sound as though the college would suffer for the association, botany was surely the least interesting discipline in academe, and she wasn't really interested anyway.

Lily's temper was rising; this was a time when Zen principles of "letting go of anger" would come in real handy.

"Heather's boy is in our beginners group."

As if on cue, a young boy ran out of the locker room, dragging his duffel bag behind him, and Lily only stopped what would have been a shockingly gauche gasp from exploding by digging her nails into her palms.

Billy junior, or someone very like what a Billy junior would look like, smiled up at them.

"Will you skate with us again tomorrow, coach?" the boy asked, breathless wonder in his voice as he looked at Billy. "You sure can skate!"

"Yeah . . . for a while anyway."

"Mom, he's way good, way better than anyone!"

"I know, darling," his mother said, swinging her glance to Billy. "Coach Bianchich is one of the best."

Lily wanted to either scream or puke at the sound of Heather's breathy tone, but she managed to refrain from either through sheer willpower, strength of character, and the mean-spirited comfort of knowing that she would be sleeping with Coach Bianchich tonight and sticky-sweet, oh-so-agreeable Heather wouldn't.

She really should rise above such pettiness. If one were truly accepting of the goodness of the world, one wouldn't even think in such narrow, despicable causal terms of triumph and advantage, winning and losing.

"You should come for dinner some night, Billy," Heather said. "Markie would enjoy it."

Obviously, the goodness of the world was a myth for Heather or perhaps she chose not to read self-help books that would put her in tune with the circle of love in the universe. Then again, maybe she preferred a more personal love.

"Boy, would I ever like it!" Markie cried. "Say you'll come, coach! I'll show you my collection of hockey cards. Hey, Mom, did you tell him about my collection?"

"I didn't get a chance to yet, Markie. We were talking about the past."

"Oh, boy. I can hardly wait. Make your lasagna, Mom! It's the best!"

"You used to like that, didn't you, Billy," Heather said, real softly.

Billy finally noticed Heather wasn't actually talking about dinner.

Jeez, Lily thought. It's about time.

"I can't promise. I'll see what I can do," he said, taking a step backward.

As if one step backward was going to hold off Heather, Lily thought. Maybe a tank might, but she wouldn't bet her life on it.

"Nice talking to you," he added and then turned to Lily. "Ready to go?"

Afraid that some completely bitchy remark was likely to fall from her lips, Lily clamped her lips shut, nodded her head, and smiled.

"What's wrong with you?" Billy said as they walked away.

He noticed that she didn't reply but he was completely blind to Heather's blatant seduction. "Nothing's wrong," Lily said, giving herself kudos for acting in a very mature, adult way when she was really highly, highly provoked. "How do you know Heather?"

"We went together for a while in high school."

"A few weeks?"

She could see him hesitating.

"A couple of years," he said. "Where are we going to eat?"

"You decide," she said, clipped and cool.

"Jeez, now you're mad. Look, I haven't seen her in years, not that it's any business of yours, Miss Lily," he reminded her. But he was smiling and trying to kiss her and he eventually succeeded because she couldn't resist. They kissed in the parking lot and then a lot more in the car until Billy said on a suffocated breath, "I'm not doing it in the car when I can have you spread-eagle on the bed in under five minutes." Lifting her back into her seat as if she didn't weigh an ounce, he pointed his finger at her and said, "Stay," in an altogether sexy-dominant way that made her even hotter than she already was.

He drove her car much too fast through town while she tried to put her clothes back in some order in case Myrtle was back from her daughter's in Biwabik. Myrtle was; her car was in her driveway. But Billy carried Lily into the house anyway, not taking no for an answer in his continuing sexy-dominant, I'm-a-man, you're-a-woman sort of way that made her so very, very ready for sex that she came the instant he entered her.

At least the first time.

And a long time later, a countless-orgasms-long-time later, they had dinner brought in.

CHAPTER **17**

The next morning, the minute Billy left for the hockey camp, Lily called Ceci and Serena and said, "I need some advice."

They met for breakfast at the Chocolate Moose, found a corner table, and once the waitress had taken their order, Ceci and Serena immediately asked, "What happened?"

"An old girlfriend."

"Ahhh . . ." they both said like ancient shamans looking at the ashes of a sacrificed bird.

"No shit," Lily said. "Now first, I know I shouldn't be hyperventilating because I shouldn't care when I've just gotten myself out of a nasty relationship and *he* has too many girlfriends to care, and this, er, thing we have going is très, très casual. But, that said, this old girlfriend's a real bitch and she's moving in like a Mack truck. She invited him to dinner. Worse, she has a boy that looks like Billy—I didn't even want to go there—and when I asked him how he knew her . . . Oh, oh, listen to this! They went together for *two years* in high school—so she's not exactly a one-night stand."

"Those long-term high school relationships," Ceci said with a grimace. "They're all wrapped up in nostalgia and lost youth and—"

"Memories of hot teenage sex," Serena added.

"Thanks," Lily said dryly.

"Sorry. I was thinking about Jerry Jerzek." Serena sighed. "He was hot."

"He couldn't have been too hot. You only went with him for a month."

Serena shrugged her cashmere-covered shoulder; it was cool that morning. "He wanted to go steady."

"The kiss of death," Ceci said with conviction.

"Not always," Lily said. "I liked Matt for a long time."

"Until you set eyes on Robbie and dumped Matt."

Lily stirred the sugar in her latte, although she'd already stirred it. "So, maybe one can't always have what one wants."

"You don't even know if you want it—him—Billy . . . whatever," Ceci said.

Lily grinned. "*It* for sure. Thanks for reminding me."

"You were the one who told me to think of these guys as a summer fling," Serena said.

Ceci restlessly tapped her fingers on the table. "If you can."

"Having withdrawal symptoms?"

"I hope that's all it is. He's only been gone a few days."

"Come over to my house. Billy's at his hockey camp every day this week."

"Why don't you both come with me to this potter's workshop near Winton? Mom wants me to pick out some of his work for the store. I just thought you'd be busy, so I didn't ask."

Workshop was a misnomer. An obvious Frank Gehry design, the pottery studio resembled the art museum in Bilbao, Spain, smaller, but just as dramatic. Set on a point overlooking Bass Lake, it reeked of money along with scenic spectacle. This potter wasn't working for the money.

Luke Manion came out to greet them—alone. No wife, no girlfriend, not even a dog. He was tall, sandy-haired, handsome in a clean-cut athletic way—soccer or lacrosse, maybe polo, although he didn't seem to keep horses. He wore sandals and shorts, a short-sleeved shirt open over his tanned chest and hard abs. He worked out or else his pots were very heavy.

He took them on a tour of his studio home with the self-deprecating casualness of the very wealthy, old-money class who drove Fords or Chevys and always had someone of lesser status manage their assets for them. It turned out he and Frank Gehry were friends, and then it turned out he and Serena had friends in common, and before the tour was over, Luke and Serena were comparing notes on art shows in Milan and Venice, skiing at Gstaad, and the best shopping on the Rue du Faubourg St.-Honoré.

He poured them a good French white, lightly chilled—the day had warmed—and then he and Serena went off to his storage room to pick out some pots.

Ceci looked at Lily and Lily looked back with raised brows as they sat on a custom-designed chartreuse linen Italian couch with a lake view.

"I think she likes him," Ceci said.

"I think they like each other or at least they go to the same art shows."

"What about Frankie?"

"You sound like his mother."

"I know his mother."

Lily gave Ceci her most mature, adult look. It was easier to be mature and objective about someone else. "You don't seriously think Serena will stay in town with Frankie, do you?"

"No."

"And he knows it too."

"That I'm not so sure about."

"Well, he'll find out soon enough."

"Sooner, rather than later, if the man with the artist's hands in there decides to make a move."

"Decides?"

"If Serena accepts, then."

But Serena seemed merely gracious to him when they returned, and even when they questioned her on the ride back to Ely she responded only casually. Maybe Luke seemed more like a brother to her with all they had in common.

CHAPTER **18**

Real disaster struck the next afternoon when Ceci went to meet Zuber on his return. He freelanced his services to several of the outfitters in town and the party he'd taken out were unloading at the Timber Trail Outfitter's docks.

In hindsight, she probably shouldn't have gone.

He hadn't asked her to.

And obviously he wasn't expecting her because the slim, tanned blonde with big tits who was draped all over him, looked like she was willing to fuck him in broad daylight.

Not that he was fighting much.

Luckily, Ceci was parked up on the hill. She'd wanted to surprise him.

So much for surprises.

When Zuber walked into her cabin an hour later, she said, "Did you take out a large party this time?"

"Naw. Just a couple of guys. One owns the Denver Broncos."

"Just two guys?" The woman had worn fishing gear—of the couture variety.

He looked up from unlacing his boots. "Something wrong?"

"Could be. Was there anyone else on your trip?"

He stopped unlacing his boots and sat up. "Meaning what?"

"Meaning I came to meet you today—stupid me—and I saw you with one of the party you didn't mention. A tanned blonde who was trying to get it on with you standing up."

"Oh, fuck . . ." His gaze shuttered.

"Care to elaborate?"

"I didn't have much choice. She was the daughter of the Broncos' owner."

"So you had to fuck her. I haven't heard that one before. Original," she said in a tight voice.

"There wasn't anywhere to hide out there. Believe me, I would have if I could."

"I don't suppose it crossed your randy mind to say no."

He blew out a breath. "Yeah, it crossed my mind."

"But not for long."

"I couldn't, okay, even if I wanted to."

"What are you? Some indentured fishing gigolo?"

"Jesus, Ceci. It was just a damned impossible situation. They got their damned fish. They're going home."

"Miss Blonde Big Tits isn't staying for a last fuck?"

"No, I told her I had a girlfriend I was going to see."

"You had one." Even as she spoke, she felt sad. He'd never said *girlfriend* before. And she was stupid enough to care.

"Are you kicking me out?"

The way he said it made her pause, but getting women was too easy for him. It always had been. "I'm kicking you out," she said, and walked into her bedroom and locked the door. The nonrational part of her brain half-hoped he'd knock on the door and plead for forgiveness.

But he didn't.

"Men can be such shits," Lily said, pouring another glass of wine for Ceci.

"You can't trust them," Serena said with a sigh, offering Ceci another ice creme wafer.

"You should have seen her," Ceci said, her eyes red from crying. "And he just took it all in. I hate giving a damn about a guy. It's so . . . so—uselessly emotional."

"Frankie said Zuber isn't himself. He only drank two beers last night."

Ceci's bloodshot gaze came up. "He was at the saloon last night?"

"Just for a short time," Serena said, trying to make up for her faux pas.

"How short a time? And don't lie. I've had all the lying I can take for a while."

"I'm not sure . . ."

"Serena!"

"An hour or so."

"Did he leave alone?"

Serena wouldn't meet her eyes.

"Don't bother, Serena," Ceci said with a sigh. "You never could lie anyway."

"I'm sorry. I didn't want to tell you."

"Who was it?"

"Don't ask me, Ceci. Please."

"If you don't tell me, I'll never speak to you again."

"You don't want to know."

"I do. Look, I could give a shit. Tell me."

Serena got busy looking for another cookie in the bag. "Miss Blonde Big Tits," she said into the bag.

Ceci shrieked.

"Frankie said she's twice divorced and used to having her way. Maybe——"

"You don't have to make excuses for Zuber. He's never turned down sex in his life," Ceci said bitterly.

"Men think with their dicks," Lily said disgustedly, and she wasn't only offering sympathy to her friend. "For instance, Billy's going to dinner at Heather's tomorrow night. He can't get out of it, he says. She invited his parents."

Ceci turned from filling her wineglass to the top. "Why didn't you say something before?"

"Because you were feeling terrible and you needed sympathy and"—Lily shrugged—"I'm so pissed I don't want to talk about it."

The phrase "I don't want to talk about it" is rhetorical. Every woman knows that. Before long, Ceci and Serena had dragged every small detail about Heather and Billy—that Lily knew—out of her.

"That's not to say there's not fifteen or so years of their *friendship*," Lily finished with a sneer, "that's outside my area of discovery."

"Oh, God. And she's divorced?" Ceci had forgotten her own problems for the moment.

"And available. You should see her glued to Billy's chest every chance she gets."

"Does he give her a chance?"

Lily made a face. "In all fairness, he's eluded her pretty well so far."

"Till dinner tomorrow night."

Lily's expression turned grim. She could practically hear the ominous *dum, da, dum, dum* of disaster. Heather's dinner was sure to be perfect— unlike *her* attempts at cooking. The conversation would be congenial and witty, with everyone in sync on all the local issues that make for ideal relationships. God knows, she couldn't fault Heather on her looks or her world-class tits. And Billy seemed dense as a post when it came to Heather's machinations. Fuck, she was screwed. "I'm screwed," she said, and held out her wineglass for a refill. "Although it shouldn't matter where he goes to dinner. Right?"

"Don't look at me," Ceci said, pouring. "I'm a basket case when it shouldn't matter to me either—who fucks whom, where."

They both turned to Serena, looking for those female words of encouragement that paper over every devastating crack in the vital structure of life, no matter how wide or deep.

"This probably isn't a good time," Serena said instead, surveying her friends with a skittish gaze. "But if we're talking about our problems . . . are we?" At their nods, she cracked an ice creme wafer in two, shoved it in her mouth, and chewed for what seemed a very long time.

"It must be bad," Ceci said.

"I don't know if it is or not," Serena finally said. "But I think it is."

"Then it is. Your gut feeling's always the true litmus test."

"Luke asked me out and I said yes."

"He did? When?"

Serena looked at her friends in amazement. "Do you practice saying things together like that?"

"Our misery puts us in sync," Lily said.

"Actually, he asked me out yesterday when we went to his studio. And then he asked me again last night, and again today. So I said yes this morning when he sent me some pink sweetheart roses in a beautiful vase he'd made."

Ceci fluttered her lashes. "The man knows how to woo."

"He knows so many of the same people I know."

"There. Just what all the relationship books say. Common interests, common goals."

"He's very nice. But so is Frankie," Serena said in a whisper.

"You're not going to tell him."

"I tried to."

"What did you tell him after he wouldn't listen?"

"I told him I had to keep you company tonight because . . . well, you know. He understood. I hope you don't mind?"

Ceci smiled. It was her first smile since Miss Blonde Big Tits had struck her retinas. "Hey, what are friends for? I'll lie through my teeth if he calls."

"Thanks, Ceci. Thanks a lot."

CHAPTER 19

It was late when Lily walked into her cabin. Billy was watching TV in the dimly lit living room.

"What are you doing here?" Her tone of voice reflected the hours of bitching about men.

"Sorry. Is it a problem?"

"You said you wouldn't be over since I was going to Ceci's."

"I figured you might come home. And look, I don't want to fight."

"Who's fighting?" But resentment vibrated in her words because she found herself thinking about Heather smiling at Billy over a perfect flower arrangement at dinner tomorrow night when it was none of her business where he ate dinner.

"Had a couple drinks, did you?"

"More than whatever comes after a couple. Do you mind?"

"Chill out. Drink all you want."

"I will," she said huffily. "And maybe I don't want to chill out. Men always want women to chill out after they've fucked someone else or are planning to fuck someone else."

"Hey, I'm not Zuber."

She looked at him lounging in her chair, male perfection in a black T-shirt and white linen slacks. "I forgot. You're not into casual sex."

He came to his feet. "You want to fight. I don't. I'll see you when you're sober." He began walking toward the door.

"How about tomorrow night?" She could have bitten her tongue the minute she spoke.

He half-turned. "Am I supposed to say yes?"

Her moment of embarrassment vanished; his voice had been ice-cold. "You're supposed to say whatever you want to say," she replied, her voice equally chill.

He opened his mouth and then shut it again.

A second later she and the ten o'clock news anchors were alone in the living room.

Oh, God—oh, Lord . . . bloody hell and damnation—maybe it wasn't Brock after all, she thought, gazing at the cookie-cutter-handsome man and the not-a-hair-out-of-place clone of a woman at his side reading from their cue cards while smiling like ventriloquists' dummies on the illuminated screen.

Maybe it was *her,* Lily. Maybe she expected too much. Maybe the search for happiness was truly a myth, like that of El Dorado.

That's what came from reading Jane Austen at too young an age, she decided, with the oversimplified logic of several glasses of wine too many. One was always expecting to find a real-life dreamscome-true Mr. Darcy. Someone virile, yet capable of tenderness, a man who had emotions beyond lust and hunting, or Monday-night football, or TV ratings, she thought with a grimace—a lover who was trustworthy and truly adored you no matter what. She was particularly looking for the beingadored part. And why not? she decided heatedly, and—even she was willing to admit—tipsily. Why *should* she relinquish the lovely concept that had been an unconscious underpinning of her emotional life since the seventh grade? She wouldn't. She didn't have to. She didn't have to do anything she didn't want, she affirmed with the megalomania of excessive drink.

She liked Mr. Darcy!

She had no intention of giving him up!

Although, strangely, the Mr. Darcy in her mind seemed to have spiky black hair tonight.

CHAPTER 20

Breakfast at the Chocolate Moose the next morning looked like a wake. Not an Irish wake where the dead were sent off to glory with a nip or two or twenty. More like a nonalcoholic Swedish wake fueled by coffee and gloom.

Even Serena wasn't able to completely enjoy the memories of her evening past; a novel, disconcerting guilt shadowed her thoughts.

"Now you're sure Frankie didn't call you?" she said for the ten thousandth time. "You'd drunk quite a bit. Maybe you don't remember."

"He didn't call," Ceci said. "No one called. No one," she added bitterly. "That's why I remember, alcoholic haze or not. *No one. Period.*"

"Did he call while you were still there, Lily?"

This, too, had not been the first query to Lily regarding this topic.

Ceci leaned across the table, clamped her hand over Serena's mouth, and spoke very slowly. "You're . . . safe . . . pussycat. Frankie . . . still . . . thinks . . . the . . . sun . . . rises . . . and . . . sets . . . on . . . you. He—did—not—call."

"I feel just terrible." Serena slumped lower on the bench built into the log wall.

Lily said, "You had fun though."

Serena's expression brightened. "Luke has a really nice sailboat."

"There you go," Ceci said, not without irony. "A nice sailboat. What more can you want?"

"I wish Frankie had a sailboat."

Ceci looked at Serena over her espresso. "Buy him one."

"I couldn't!"

"Sure you could. And you could teach him to sail. Maybe he could learn about those shops in Paris too."

Serena stuck her tongue out. "Now you're being mean."

"Just tell him you're going to see other men. Everyone's a commitmentphobe now anyway," Lily said. "He'll probably be relieved."

"I should."

"Then you can see Luke *and* Frankie. How *is* Luke in bed, by the way?"

Serena blushed. "I . . . didn't—I mean . . . I didn't feel like it. And he was a perfect gentleman."

"And obviously not from the Range," Ceci said. "Men here feel obliged to fuck everything in sight."

A small silence ensued.

"Let's not get too righteous," Lily quietly said. "None of us has exactly taken religious orders. In fact—"

"I know, I know," Ceci said with a sigh. "Look, I was just giving you advice a few days ago, about getting back on that horse. So, who's up for dancing tonight?"

Dancing tonight was on the same short list with driving a rusty stake through her heart, Lily thought, but Ceci was staring at her, waiting, and she was her friend. She nodded yes.

"I'll tell Frankie to meet me there." Serena patted Ceci's hand. "We're going to have fun."

Mentally groaning, Lily forced her mouth into a smile. But that's the best she could do. No way could she actually say the word *fun*.

CHAPTER **21**

"It was such a surprise to hear from Heather again," Billy's mother said, stuffing some extra Kleenex in her purse. It was a habit, like keeping chains in the trunk of one's car even though radial tires had been on the market for thirty years, a habit left over from when her children were young. Marlene Bianchich cast a quick glance at her son, who was standing at the door, holding it open. Maybe this dinner invitation tonight meant she'd be having some new grandchildren soon.

"Heather's been picking up her kid at hockey camp and asking me over," Billy said. "I finally said yes." The edited version of Heather's WWF no-holds-barred persistence.

"Well, that was nice of you. Wasn't that nice, Harold?"

Billy's father was trying to watch the last few minutes of the news. He never missed the news. Except, possibly, for funerals and weddings, and even then you could sometimes find him in a corner trying to pick up a signal on his Sony Watchman.

"Harold! We're going to be late!"

Sighing, Billy's father clicked the remote, the TV screen went black, and he rose from his Barca-lounger—the only piece of furniture in the house that was his, although only after a protracted struggle with his wife's aesthetic principles.

Great, Billy thought. We're off to a good start.

"Harold, you remember Heather was always right on time. She was one of those young girls who was very punctual. Hurry now."

With a long-suffering look, Mr. Bianchich picked up his sport jacket from the back of the chair where his wife had put it and moved toward the door.

"Won't this be fun! Did I tell you Heather's mother came into the store today?"

Billy often only half-listened to his mother because she liked to tell him about what someone wore thirty years ago, or what she'd eaten in about the same time frame, and she liked to give advice. He didn't care about thirty years ago and her advice always had to do with him marrying. But the words *Heather's mother* set his warning antennae on full alert. Shit. I suppose they'd spent time picking out the place for the wedding reception and planning the menu.

Sometimes it really didn't pay to be polite.

He should have told Heather—He tried to think of something that would have deterred her and came up blank.

He glanced at his watch as they walked to the car.

It was going to be a long evening.

Billy braced himself as they walked up the brick path to Heather's house. He felt as though he should be armed or at least wearing Kevlar when he was going to be up against not only Heather's determined assault but his mother's crusade to marry him off. He'd stay two hours, he thought. That should be sufficient for politesse. Then he'd leave for some yet-to-be-manufactured appointment and make sure he had an ironclad excuse for any future dinner invitations.

But Heather threw him off from the moment she opened the door. She was polite, but not effusive, welcoming them with casual friendliness. She and his mother went off to the kitchen, leaving Billy and his father with her son and several boxes of Markie's hockey card collection. Heather brought out beer in chilled, frosty glasses for the men, turned on the TV news for Harold, smiled at her son who was showing his favorite hockey card to Billy, and then returned to the kitchen. If Billy didn't know better, he would have relaxed. But her behavior reminded him of the innocuous scenes in a scary movie—the ones just before something dis-astrous happens.

He was on edge by the time they were called to dinner. Everyone else seemed in convivial spirits. Markie was always happy when someone would listen to him talk about his collection. Billy's father had watched the entire *NewsHour with Jim Lehrer,* had drunk two beers, and hadn't been asked to converse. For him, what wasn't to like about the evening? The steady buzz of conversation from the kitchen implied a harmonious degree of rapport between the women, verified by their arm-in-arm pose as they stood in the dining room doorway waiting for the men to join them.

Billy felt a strong inclination to bolt at that cozy image.

His mother waved everyone to their places and began slicing the lasagna as though it was her dinner, as though they were all one big happy family.

The hairs on the back of Billy's neck began to rise.

But Heather didn't speak to him directly, choosing to converse to the table at large. Markie talked about hockey, his questions directed to Billy. Mr. Bianchich, true to form, confined his remarks to such phrases as "Pass the salt" and "Yes, I'll have another serving," while Mrs. Bianchich offered anecdotes of a local nature for their amusement.

The lasagna was excellent, as was the wine. Heather had made Italian bread as well. Dessert was a wild blueberry pie for which she apologized because the berries were frozen. The new crop wasn't ripe yet, she explained. She was hoping the homemade vanilla ice cream would help make up for that shortcoming.

"Isn't Heather the best cook?" Marlene exclaimed, beaming at their hostess.

"It was nothing," Heather demurred, looking suitably modest.

The required praise was immediately forthcoming, not that it wasn't merited.

After accepting their compliments, Heather suggested they have coffee on the back porch. "The fireflies are so beautiful at night," she said with a sweet smile.

Everything was perfect.

Way too perfect.

Even his father wasn't in any hurry to go home, Billy thought. Now if only he was interested in a woman like Heather who could cook, act with Academy Award flare, and manipulate with Machiavellian ease. If only he wasn't enamored of a woman who couldn't cook to save her life, wore her feelings on her sleeve, and couldn't manipulate her way out of a paper bag. With thoughts of Lily beginning to rev up his libido, Billy quickly drank his coffee and Amaretto while Heather put Markie to bed. When she returned he rose from his chair. "Thanks for everything," he said. "But I have to be at the rink early tomorrow, so we'd better go."

"Have another coffee," his mother said. "It's still early. I have to help Heather with the dishes yet."

"If Billy has to leave, I could drive you home, Mr. and Mrs. Bianchich," Heather offered. "More Amaretto and coffee, Mr. Bianchich? The late news will be on in ten minutes."

It was getting way too creepy.

"Thanks again for dinner," Billy said, backing toward the doorway to the kitchen. "See you tomorrow."

He walked through the kitchen, down the hall, out the front door and onto the stoop, where he stood for a moment in the darkness, feeling as though he'd escaped a trap, his tension melting away.

A slow smile lifted the corners of his mouth.

Now to find Lily and see if she was still talking to him.

CHAPTER **22**

While Billy had been dining at Heather's, the women had been taking in the convivial atmosphere at the Birch Lake Saloon. In summer, every night was like spring break. The joint was jumping.

Ceci was determined to forget Zuber and wasn't having any difficulty luring interested parties. She wore a white cotton Michael Kors corset dress that laced up the back, and all the unattached as well as some attached men were dreaming of unlacing those red silk ties. As the evening progressed, it looked as though the band's drummer was going to get lucky. Ceci was seated between his outspread legs and he was drumming around her—with the dexterity that skill, talent, and several lines of coke produced. She seemed to be enjoying herself, if the heated kisses they exchanged between numbers were any indication. He obviously was. When he rose occasionally to take a bow, his hard-on was conspicuous.

Lily sat with Frankie and Serena. They were busy whispering to each other and Lily was busy deterring the various men who came up to ask her to dance. What one didn't do for one's friends, she thought, having sent the umpteenth man off with some polite refusal. Glancing at her watch, she decided she could leave in twenty minutes without appearing rude to Ceci. Not that Ceci seemed to be noticing while she had her mouth glued to the drummer's lips. Looking up, she saw Luke making his way through the crowd and tried to catch Serena's eye to give her warning. But Serena was looking at Frankie and smiling her I'm-in-love smile.

This was one of those times when Lily would have liked to run and hide.

Luke stopped at their booth, his gaze on Serena. "I thought I might find you here."

Frankie looked at Luke, then at Serena who had gone pale, then back to Luke. He held out his hand. "Frankie Aronson," he said, his voice neutral.

"Luke Manion."

The men shook hands.

"Mind if I join you?" Without waiting for an answer, Luke sat down beside Lily.

"Drink?" At Luke's nod, Frankie waved for a waitress.

If she had just left five minutes ago, Lily thought, taking note of Frankie's cool gaze.

While Luke waited for his drink, they discussed the band and the crowds that descended on the town each summer. Once the waitress came with his gin and tonic, Luke looked directly at Serena. "I'm having a few people out tomorrow night. You should come."

"I'm not sure . . . that is," Serena stammered. "We have plans."

"That's your studio on Bass Lake, isn't it?" Frankie turned from Luke to Serena. "Doesn't your mom carry Luke's work in her store?"

"Yes . . . that is—I mean . . . yes."

"Serena drove over and picked out some of my pots a couple days ago," Luke said. "We went sailing yesterday," he added, in his take-no-prisoners offensive.

"I see." Frankie's expression was unreadable. "Did you have a good breeze on the lake?"

"An excellent one. You should come with us sometime."

Frankie didn't answer. He said instead, "Do you ever race in the Lake of the Woods Regatta?"

"I've gone twice."

"My cousins and I were my uncle's grunts on his J-30. That's a dangerous course."

"You sail?" The faintest disparagement echoed in Luke's tone.

"A little."

"You'll have to come out and try my keelboat." Challenge infused every syllable.

Frankie ran into contentious men every week, sometimes every day. He didn't have anything to prove anymore. "Probably not. But thanks for the invitation."

Luke's mouth tightened. "Care to dance, Serena?"

"No, thank you. I'm here with Frankie." Looking at him, she offered him a tentative smile.

"Go and dance. I'll wait."

"I don't want to."

Even when he was seated, Frankie's size was formidable. He smiled at Luke. "I guess you'll have to find another partner tonight."

As if Luke's appearance wasn't disconcerting enough, Mr. Dockers chose that moment to pull up a chair and plunk himself down. "What's everyone drinking?" he inquired cheerfully, winking at Lily and waving over a waitress. "You all look like you need a drink."

The ensuing conversation was stilted, although Mr. Dockers didn't notice because he was on vacation, he'd been drinking since afternoon, and he preferred the sound of his own voice. It took all Lily's diplomacy to refuse his repeated invitations to dance, and when he left briefly to request a song from the band, she took the opportunity to escape.

If Ceci and Serena were still in need of her company, she was sorry. She was no longer in the mood to be polite. Try as she might, she'd not been able to distract her thoughts from Billy and Heather.

It was almost midnight. Heather must have him in bed by now.

CHAPTER **23**

Billy practically walked into Zuber when he entered the saloon because Zuber was more or less blocking the entrance. He looked grim. Scanning the room, Billy took note of Ceci seated on the drummer's lap.

It looked like payback time.

He surveyed the booths lining the walls next, searching for Lily. There was Serena, Frankie, the rich potter—Luke something—and Mr. Dockers all together in a booth.

No Lily.

"Not a good night for either one of us," Billy muttered, thinking Lily had already left with someone.

"It depends," Zuber said, not taking his eyes from Ceci, his voice flint-hard.

"We need a drink first." Billy knew what that tone of voice implied.

"Or ten." Zuber's scowl had deepened. Ceci was kissing the drummer.

"Or twenty. I just came from dinner at Heather's—*with* my parents."

Zuber's gaze swiveled to Billy. "For real?"

"I could have sold tickets. Heather was playing the small-town-girl-next-door-meets-Martha-Stewart-doing-Americana."

Even under duress, Zuber couldn't help but smile. "You're shittin' me. Heather?"

"In the flesh. We had blueberry pie and home-made ice cream."

"Twenty bucks says her mother made them."

"You're probably right, but I'm not getting near enough to ask. Speaking of near—" He nodded toward Ceci melting into the drummer.

"I'm thinking about kicking some butt," Zuber said in a low growl.

"She might not like it."

"I wasn't planning on asking her whether she did or not. Asshole prick drummer is poaching."

"If you're serious about *poaching,* you *really* need a drink. Come on."

Zuber didn't move.

"Now," Billy said, dragging Zuber toward the bar. But they hadn't walked more than a dozen steps when Zuber broke away and made for the bandstand.

Billy followed in case he needed help.

Halfway to the bandstand, Frankie stepped into Zuber's path and put out his hand. "Easy now," he said, knowing what Zuber could do in a brawl. "Les and Larry don't want you breaking up their bar."

"I'm not touching their bar. Out of my way."

It was surprising how fast the Siminich brothers could move if they had to. "Come on, man." Les tucked a handful of joints into Zuber's shirt pocket. "Mellow out. Try this good Thai."

"The band's done in fifteen minutes anyway," Larry said. "You can take care of business then."

Billy added his brawn to the barricade. "It's not worth it, Nick."

All four men had deliberately placed themselves between Zuber and the band so Ceci was no longer in Zuber's line of vision.

For a second no one moved. No one spoke. A sea of noise washed over them. Then Les clicked his Bic and lifted the lighter toward Zuber.

Another breath-held moment passed.

Zuber reached into his shirt pocket, pulled out a joint, stuck it in his mouth, and leaned toward the fluttering flame.

Much later, when Billy and Zuber emerged from the Siminiches' office, it took a moment for their eyes to adjust to the gloom. The saloon was empty; only the neon beer lights illuminated the large space.

"What the hell," Zuber murmured. "You can't win 'em all."

"You got that right."

"Live and let live."

"Whatever."

Ganja eloquence in action.

Zuber looked at Billy. "Goin' home?"

Billy shrugged. "Maybe. You?"

"Nah."

"Need any help?"

Zuber smiled. "Nah. Make love, not war, that's my motto."

Billy laughed. "Sounds good to me."

CHAPTER 24

Zuber wasn't quiet entering Ceci's cabin. Nor was he particularly slow-gaited, regardless of the amount of weed he'd smoked. He arrived on the screened porch before the drummer was fully out of bed.

"Damn you, Zuber!" Ceci cried, jumping up and standing like a nude avenger between Zuber and the blonde-haired drummer. "Don't you dare take another step!"

"I don't want any trouble, man," Zuber said, real mellowlike. "And nothin' against you, but the lady here is— Hey, you don't have to run out without putting on your clothes, Jesus, stop a second . . . I really liked that one song you played—that one that sounded like outer space there in that middle part— Hey, your shoes, man . . . don't forget your shoes." A half-smile played across his lips as Zuber gently rocked on his boot soles. "Nice guy," he said, surveying the drummer's fleeing form. "Fast . . . he's real fast."

A moment later, the slammed door echoed out on the porch.

"WHAT THE FUCK DO YOU THINK YOU'RE DOING!"

Zuber leaned back. "Hey, don't shout. I'm real close."

"GET THE FUCK OUT!" Ceci shouted.

But Zuber dropped onto the bed instead and lay sprawled on his back.

"DAMN YOU, GET OUT!" Ceci was quivering with rage. "DO YOU HEAR ME?"

He smiled at her. "The whole lake heard. Maybe clear-into-town heard."

"You're not staying here! You're not! You're not! You're *not*!" She dragged on his arm.

He didn't budge.

When she began pummeling him with her fists, he grabbed her around the waist, hoisted her over him and dropped her on the wall side of the bed.

Scrambling up, she socked him in the face with all her might.

He shook his head and took a breath. "Jeez, relax." But as she was winding up for another shot, he moved with amazing speed and suddenly she was flat on her back on the bed, her arms at her sides, Zuber's long fingers encircling her wrists. "Don't hit me," he whispered, leaning in close. "I'm in this real good mood."

"I'm in this real hellish mood in case you didn't notice. This isn't Zuber's Holiday Inn Central. You have to MAKE A FUCKING RESERVATION, YOU PRICK!"

"Sorry," he said, blinking against the blast of her voice. "I forgot to call."

"You also forgot to keep your dick in your pants last night and the night before and the night before that!"

"Look, I'm sorry about—well . . . everything."

"Yeah, me too. Real fucking sorry."

"I've missed you."

She glared at him. "I was home last night. You didn't call."

He shut his eyes briefly and exhaled. "Sorry again." Releasing her wrists, he sat up on the edge of the bed and rubbed his hand over his eyes. "What do you want me to do?" A seriousness infused his voice, the ganja mellowness gone.

"Why don't you jump off a fucking bridge." Ceci sighed. "A low one maybe. Shit, I don't know what you should do—I don't know what *I* should do."

He glanced at her over his shoulder. "I'll promise to be—"

"Don't snow me, Zuber. I didn't fall off the last turnip truck, for Christ's sake."

"Look, I'll try to be better. How's that? I'll try—really."

She scowled. "You're still going to pay big time."

"Just name it."

She'd drunk too much tonight; she'd danced too

much. She'd expended too much energy on revenge. "Later," Ceci said. "I'm too tired to be creative."

"Mind if I lie down?"

"Sure, why not. You scared off Doug."

"Don't say it like that."

"Like what?"

"Like any dick will do."

"Don't go there, Zuber. You of all people don't stand a prayer with that moral argument."

He blew out a breath. "Point taken."

"You bet your ass, point taken."

"Whatever you say. I don't want to fight." He wasn't straight enough to argue and it was real low on his list of priorities anyway. He began unbuttoning his shirt.

When he pulled off his short-sleeved plaid shirt, Ceci saw the scratches on his back and all her anger came flooding back with a vengeance. "Get out," she said, her voice like ice.

He turned around. "What did I do now?"

"Take those fucking scratches on your back and yourself and get out of my house."

"Oh, shit," he said under his breath.

"Hard to keep track, isn't it? With so many women to fuck you never know who's going to be mad about what." She climbed out of bed and he didn't try to stop her. Grabbing a quilt, she walked into the bedroom, shut the door, and crawled into bed. She didn't like sleeping in the bedroom; she couldn't see the lake. But she couldn't deal with Zuber.

Not now.

Not when she wanted him, scratches and all.

CHAPTER 25

B illy had considered the possibility Lily had
gone home with someone when he'd not seen
her at the saloon. He'd not considered what to do if
she had. When he saw the car with Illinois plates
parked in her drive, he wondered if it might be her
ex-husband's.

He should leave.

But he turned off the truck lights instead, got
out of the truck and stood in the shadows like a
stalker, watching Lily and a man sitting across from
her in her living room drink wine and talk.

Who was he? When had he come? How long was
he staying? The impulse to intrude into Lily's living
room and ask her was intense. But he was more
cautious than Zuber or perhaps the newness of
their relationship deterred him. He'd been sleeping

with Lily only a few days; he had no right to take issue with her friends. Reason notwithstanding, he was pissed and came close to knocking at her door a dozen times.

He didn't though. Too many women wanting more than he was willing to give had made him wary. He was eminently practical about involvement.

He continued to watch though, until they finally went to bed, his breathing arrested for the moments it took Lily to show the man to his room. When she closed the door on her guest and walked into her own bedroom, he started breathing again.

But he waited outside because he didn't trust any man in such proximity to Lily.

He waited an hour. Like an infatuated adolescent, he thought. Then he waited a half hour more.

Just to make sure.

CHAPTER 26

Frankie and Serena were lying on their backs—not touching—trying not to let each other know they were awake. They'd returned to Frankie's without speaking about Luke, they'd made love without speaking about Luke, and now they lay in the darkness thinking about not talking about Luke.

Serena sneezed.

Frankie could have said, "Are you awake?" but he didn't. He sighed, an unconscious, muted sound.

"I can't not talk about this!" Serena blurted out.

He pretended to be sleeping.

"I'm going to take that gun, weapon, pistol—whatever you call that thing in that holster over there—and shoot it if you don't say something! I know you're not sleeping!" she exclaimed in an exasperated tone he'd never heard before.

He still pretended to sleep.

She threw her legs over the side of the bed and began to rise.

"I'm awake."

She swung around. "I want to talk about—"

"The guy with the sailboat?"

"Yes." She couldn't quite bring herself to say his name either.

"I don't have any hold on you. See whomever you want." His voice was hard and flat.

"If you're angry, say so. Talk to me."

"There's nothing to talk about. You'll be gone at the end of the summer and I'll still be here. You don't like Ely and I do. What do you want to discuss?"

Tears came to her eyes. "I don't know," she said in a tiny voice.

He looked at her for a three count and then he sat up in a graceful flow of honed muscle, pulled her into his arms and rolled back down. "Don't cry," he whispered, holding her close. "I want you to stay. I just don't think you will. So I'm not getting my hopes up."

"I'm really sorry about Luke," she said, sniffling away her tears, her eyes huge as she looked up at him. "He's nice, but he's not you."

Frankie smiled. "He's about five million dollars not me."

"I don't care about the money."

"Sure you do. But that's okay. I have things I care about too."

"Everyone thinks I'm mercenary . . . and—and . . . shallow and—"

"I like you just the way you are," he said softly. "You're perfect."

"I could stay in Ely . . . I'm pretty sure I could."

"Let's not worry about that right now. I'm happy with one day at a time."

"You're sure?" She sighed. "I'm sort of a one-day-at-a-time person myself."

He knew. That's why she never stayed anywhere long. "Good," he said. "That works out fine, then. We're both one-day-at-a-time kind of people."

"I'm in love with you, you know."

His heart did a little side-step lurch.

"Did you hear me?"

He took a small breath. "Yeah."

"Do you love me?"

He didn't answer.

Serena wasn't used to men not loving her. She frowned, her bottom lip pushed out in a small pout.

Frankie smoothed away her frown with the pad of his forefinger. "For what it's worth, I love you."

"That's not very romantic." She wrinkled her nose. "I've never told anyone I loved them before."

He didn't want to be cynical, but a man in his job got to be whether he wanted to or not. If she loved him, he doubted it would be for long. "I love you oceans deep and mountains high, till the rocks melt with the sun . . ." he said softly, mixing his poets, meaning every word.

Her smile warmed the darkness along with his heart.

"That's so sweet," she whispered. "I just know

everything's going to work out. It's so much fun being in love. It's so much fun making love to you," she
added in a low, sultry purr. "And speaking about
making love—would you mind . . . I know it's
late—but if you—"

He stopped her words with a kiss, and when his
mouth lifted from hers, they were both having fun
again.

It was different making love when the actual word
love had been exchanged with a significance separate
from the casual words *about* love. There seemed to be
a new depth, a permanence to their relationship, a vir-
tual reality land of adulthood neither had ever entered before. And like new pilgrims to the land of milk
and honey they were filled with joy and well-being.

"Tell me you love me again," Serena whispered,
her arms wrapped around Frankie's neck, the
rhythm of their bodies melding in a blissful flux
and flow. "Tell me a hundred times more . . ."

"Two hundred times, kitten. Ten thousand
times—I love you," he said, low and heated, the
words coming easily now, his reservations appeased
by pleasure, by carnal bewitchment, his libido over-
riding any concerns about Serena's constancy.

"I've never felt like this . . . oh, God—like that . . .
oh, Frankieee . . ."

She was right, he thought, the top of his head
beginning to lift away. These feelings were damn near
unimaginable even two weeks ago. Lord Almighty,
she was moving in just the right way . . . oh,
fuuuck . . .

CHAPTER **27**

When Ceci woke in the morning, she saw Zuber, sleeping in a chair he'd pulled up to the bed, his jaw shadowed with dark stubble. His shirt was buttoned up to his neck, his long legs were propped on the bed. A folded piece of paper lay in his lap, her name printed in bold letters on its face.

He woke when she picked it up.

Unfolding the note, she read, *I'll pay whatever you want. You're the boss.* As if, she thought, but she couldn't help but smile. Besides, it was a gorgeous morning, Zuber was gorgeous as ever, and she needed sex.

Her brows arched in query. "Anything?"

"Yep."

No equivocation there. "What if I have a long list?"

"We'll start at the top."

He'd meant it literally, but his tone suggested more, a subconscious intonation he immediately apologized for. "I just like being with you," he explained. "I have for a long time. In fact, I almost wrote to you a couple times last winter."

"Almost?"

He shrugged. "Cold feet, I suppose. No longer a problem," he quickly amended. "No cold feet or hands or any other body part." He half-smiled. "In fact . . ."

"I noticed."

"It's up to you, of course. Under the circumstances, with me in deep-shit trouble and all, it's completely up to you."

"That shirt looks kind of tight buttoned up so high."

"No way I'm taking this off for at least a week."

"It's going to get wet when we take a bath together."

"Of course, if you want me to take it off, I will," he said with a flash of a smile.

"Maybe I could wash that bitch's nail marks off your back."

"Be my guest."

"And I get to boss you around for a week— seven days total—whenever you're in town."

"Not in public."

"Damn right in public."

He grimaced. "Are you gonna embarrass me?"

"You betcha."

He was silent for a moment, lips pursed, thinking. "But we get to take a bath now, right?"

She nodded.

He came to his feet and grinned. "You've got a deal."

She stretched lazily. "I like my bathwater warm, but not too warm."

"I remember."

"And no bubble bath."

"You got it. I hate the taste of soap."

"And some orange juice. I'd like some orange juice first."

"Okeydokey."

She smiled. "Aren't you going to complain even a little?"

"Do I look stupid? I'm five minutes from fucking you. Or, knowing you, more like three minutes."

But it turned out to be ten minutes because the water pipes at the cabin were old and the water trickled into the tub like those oasis streams in the Sahara he'd seen on his bicycle trek across Africa. But if he'd waited for Ceci all night, he could wait a few minutes more, and he wasn't about to complain considering she'd decided to forgive him. He briefly winced at the word *forgive*—formerly an alien word in his world. Then he said, "What the fuck," under his breath . . . the Zuber short form of therapy . . . and poured himself a large glass of orange juice too.

Since patience had never been Ceci's strong suit,

she went into the bathroom when the tub was only half full, stood on the threshold unconsciously tapping her finger on the doorjamb, fidgeting from foot to foot. "It's way past five minutes," she complained.

"Drink your juice," he said, pointing at it without turning around. He was putting two towels on the rack over the tub.

"I don't feel like it right now."

"Then I'll drink it."

She watched him narrow the spacing between the towels and suddenly wondered how well she really knew Zuber, even after the ultimate intimacies they'd shared. But he swung around and smiled at her and she knew all she had to know.

No one turned her on like Zuber.

The complexities swept aside by her need for instant gratification, she said, "That's enough water." Dropping her robe on the floor, she moved toward him.

Zuber had his shorts off by the time she covered the small distance between them, and when she reached up to undo his shirt, he didn't even hesitate. He helped pull free the buttons, although he prudently handed her into the tub before he took off his shirt. And he kept his back to the wall as he stepped into the tub.

She noticed and grinned. "You're really sweet."

"Yeah, right." Sitting down, he slid into a sprawl, his long legs bent double in her vintage claw-foot tub. "Self-preservation, babe."

"Or appeasement."

Appeasement wasn't a word he was comfortable with, but he knew better than to disagree. "How's the water temperature, ma'am?" he said instead. "Is it to your liking?"

"Along with everything else I see," she murmured, sliding her foot up the inside of his leg. She was facing Zuber, her back to the faucet, his proximity doing the usual things to her libido. "Now what do I want you to do first," she teased. "Seeing how I've a week of orders to give."

He softly groaned.

"You said I could."

He gave her one of those I-didn't-think-you-meant-it looks.

"Or if you like, we could forget about it."

"Forget about what?" he asked cautiously.

"Sex."

"I was afraid that was what you meant. So give me some orders."

"You sound reluctant."

"*Please, pretty please,* give me some orders."

"That's better."

He glared at her. "I'm not sure she was worth it," he grumbled.

Ceci's brows rose. "I wouldn't know."

He exhaled in a long, slow sigh of resignation. "Tell me what you want."

"How about a little enthusiasm."

The look he gave her made her reconsider. "Then

again, *enthusiasm* might not be the right word," she said smoothly. "Maybe the word I want is—"

"Top-bench-in-the-sauna hot sex . . . is that one word?" Leaning forward, he scooped her up and deposited her on his lap as though she were weightless, when in fact she would never be a size eight again. Actually, she'd never been a size eight—which thought was abruptly dismissed from her brain when Zuber's rock-hard penis slipped inside her, his palms closed over her hips, and riveting sensation took the place of highly superfluous reflection.

"Then there's times I don't want to be the boss," she purred long moments later as he slowly raised her for the next glorious downstroke.

His dark eyes were only inches away. "I know," he said, his voice like velvet, the sleek internal friction exquisite, sovereignty and dominion whisper soft. "I know what you like . . ."

CHAPTER **28**

Billy had dialed Lily's number twice that morning, but hung up before it started ringing. After that, he pulled himself together, went to work, and tried not to think of the man she was probably sitting across from at the breakfast table.

That exercise in futility didn't last long.

He picked up the phone in the back of the store and dialed her number again.

"Billy! Look who's here!" His mother's voice rang down the plumbing aisle and he looked up. Fuck. He slammed down the phone.

Heather waved at him, Heather's mother waved at him. He glanced at his watch. It was seven-fucking-thirty!

"Billy! Come up to the front and say good morning!" his mother cried.

It wasn't a good morning. It was a fucked morning. Lily may have slept with the guy from Illinois—maybe her ex . . . not a pleasant thought. He was going nuts with jealousy when he'd never been jealous in his life. And now—smiling Heather and her smiling mother and *his* smiling mother. He knew how a trapped animal felt, he thought, walking toward them.

"Mrs. Drollet has invited us to share their table at the hockey pancake breakfast next Saturday. Isn't that nice?"

"I told Mom you wouldn't want to sit through some silly program with all the hockey kids and their parents," Heather said with artful treachery.

"Of course he wouldn't mind," Mrs. Bianchich said. "We've always supported the pancake breakfast."

"I'm not sure, Mom. I think Zuber and I are going up to Whitefish that day."

"Nonsense. You never miss a pancake breakfast. We must have gone to— Let me think . . . you were six when we first went and now—"

"If you have plans, Billy, I'll tell Markie he can sit by you some other year." Heather gave him a sad little smile. "He was so looking forward to sitting with his coach."

"Billy." His mother was looking at him through narrowed eyes.

There was no escape. "Maybe Zuber and I could leave after the breakfast," he said.

His mother's smile was instant. "We'll meet you

girls and Markie at City Hall at nine then. Harold always enjoys the pancakes too."

"You're so sweet, Billy. Thanks." Heather's smile was too smug for Billy's peace of mind. "See you at hockey camp this afternoon. Markie can't stop talking about you—how you played with him last night and knew all the players on his cards and were just so, well, *great.*"

"We really enjoyed ourselves, didn't we, Billy. You have quite a cook for a daughter, Ethel. Even homemade ice cream. My word!"

Luckily Billy wasn't required to respond for the mothers launched into an exchange of ice-cream recipes, giving Billy his opportunity to flee.

Heather was going to be a problem now that she was back in town. Although he could understand why Charlie Trumble took up with his secretary and moved to Duluth. Heather was damned annoying.

In the quiet of the storage room, he took a few moments to bemoan his pancake-breakfast fate. He was going to have to have a plain, hardball talk with his mother. She could like Heather all she wanted. But he wasn't playing that game.

CHAPTER **29**

Tom Schaumberg was one of the lawyers who had helped Lily with her divorce. Last spring, when he'd expressed some interest in seeing Ely, she'd politely invited him to visit sometime, never expecting he would.

She'd been more than surprised to find him parked in her driveway on her return to the cabin last evening. So much for casual invitations.

But he'd been pleasant company over a glass of wine and a perfect gentleman. He was planning on staying a day or so, if it was all right with her, he'd said. Then he was meeting a party at Giant's Ridge for a golf tournament. She'd declined his invitation to join them. It was all very civilized.

And she'd missed Billy every minute of the evening.

Would he call? she wondered when she woke. *Had* he called last night? She'd have to get an answering machine; it was no longer a low-level priority. She wanted to *know* if he'd called. Although maybe he'd had a splendid evening at Heather's and he'd never call again. She shouldn't care. If he didn't want to call, he didn't have to call. She was a mature, capable, take-charge-of-her-life kind of woman who could very well do without a man who wasn't truly interested.

Even if he was fantastic in bed—no doubt because of those legendary muscles, although one couldn't discount the issue of stamina, or, more important—despite all the platitudes to the contrary—his rather remarkable size.

She dragged the phone into bed, pulled the covers over her head, and phoned Ceci, who could be counted on to put everything into perspective regarding sex and the usefulness or superficial convenience/utilitarian function of men. Which would be very helpful right now when she was in this frenzy of longing.

Zuber answered the phone. Fine. Great. Ceci and Zuber made up. She was the only one without a man. Which she may or may not have snappishly noted in greeting.

"You're grumpy," Ceci said.

"I'm not grumpy. I'm sexually deprived," Lily replied, hypersensitive and fretful. "You obviously had a glorious night and I'm sure Serena did, while I slept alone."

"Call him."

"No! He was the one who went to dinner with his old girlfriend."

"Who cares? Call him and invite him over. Hockey camp doesn't start till one."

Lily sighed. "Even if I wanted to, I have company."

"In bed?"

"No, not in bed. If I had someone in bed, I wouldn't be sexually deprived."

"Who's over?"

"This is very strange." And Lily went on to explain her visitor.

"I'll tell Zuber so Billy knows. I think he was looking for you last night."

"He was?" The world suddenly took on a golden glow. There was no rational explanation. "When?"

"Late. I wasn't exactly sober, so I'm not sure."

"You and Zuber made up."

"We have an agreement. Don't we, Nick?"

"That sounds interesting. You'll have to tell me sometime when you can talk."

"Nick, don't"—Ceci giggled— "I gotta go. Call Billy right now."

Lily wanted to. She flipped back the covers and glanced at the clock. Almost eight. He'd be at the store. She didn't want to leave her room to find the phone book and maybe run into Tom, so she called information and rang up the store. Billy's mother answered and Lily had to respond to a dozen questions about her parents before she was able to get Billy's cell phone number. She felt as if she was back in junior high, huddled under her covers so her voice wouldn't carry. She dialed his number. One-two-three; she counted the rings. Answer, don't be at Heather's. Four-five. He's not going to answer, hang up before you look like a fool. Six-seven.

"Hello."

His voice sounded wonderful—deep, deliciously male—perfect. She couldn't speak. She opened her mouth but only a croak came out.

"Lily, is that you?"

How mortifying. She cleared her throat. "Hello." That was original.

"Where are you? You sound muffled."

She couldn't say she was under the covers. "I'm at home."

"I'll be over in ten minutes."

There was a god. "You can't," she quickly said. "I have company."

"Who the hell is he?"

"Did you talk to Zuber already?"

"Not since last night."

"How did you know it was a he?"

"Never mind. I'll meet you at my place then—in ten minutes. I miss you."

Surely those were some of the most beautiful words in the world. "I don't know if I can get away."

"I'll make you come till you cry uncle."

"It might take me a bit longer than ten minutes. I'll have to leave him a note."

"Hurry," Billy said, husky and low. "I'm going crazy."

She threw on some clothes, wrote a note for Tom, tiptoed down the hall, left the note on the kitchen table, and quietly let herself out of the cabin. Then she ran down the driveway like some lovesick pathetic woman who couldn't live without her man.

At the base of her drive where it met the gravel road Billy stood waiting.

It felt like one of those slow-motion-running-toward-each-other commercials except that the green pasture with daisies was missing and the slow-motion part was missing and they didn't meet in the dead-center middle of the frame because Billy was sprinting all out. They met closer to the cabin than the road and fell into each other's arms within sight of Myrtle Carlson, who had been watching out her window all morning. She'd been curious about the car with Illinois plates parked in Lily's drive.

Everyone in town had heard about Brock and the nasty divorce. Myrtle felt it was her Christian duty to stand guard in case Lily needed some help what with her parents out of town and all.

Now wasn't that nice. It looked as though Lily didn't need her help after all.

Myrtle reached for her phone.

"You were right. I shouldn't have gone," Billy murmured, hugging Lily. "You have to come with me to the pancake breakfast . . . just say yes," he added when she looked perplexed.

"Yes," she said, willing to agree to any kind of invitation he might offer. "And I shouldn't have snapped at you yesterday."

He took a step back and smiled at her. "I don't mind, really. I should have listened to you and I could have avoided the most miserable evening of my life. I went looking for you afterward."

"I wish you had found me. I missed you." She didn't care that it wasn't wise to lay bare your feelings on such short acquaintance. She didn't care that she was violating every chic rule for dating and getting your man. She didn't even care that she was violating her own decision about no involvement so soon after her divorce. After last night, she meant it big time.

"So who's the guy?" Billy tried to keep his tone casual and failed. Last night had transformed his rules against involvement as well. Not that he'd admit it, but he was watching her like an FBI interrogator, looking for subterfuge.

"Nobody . . . I mean, he was my lawyer for the divorce, that's all." She went on to explain, Billy's expression lightening with each word.

"You're free then."

"For a couple of hours at least."

"Do you mind walking? My truck was parked behind the storage buildings and I didn't want to take the time to get it." He grinned. "I ran here."

There were those perfect moments in life and this was one of them. He'd run to her. It was going to be hard to top that one.

Little did she know.

An hour later, forty-five minutes of which had been spent in a delirium of lovemaking, they came up for air. Billy wiped the sweat from his face on the pillowcase. Even Lily was sweating and she hardly ever perspired. Although that, along with so many things, had changed since she met Billy. Such as understanding the true meaning of bliss. Or viewing Ceci's unrestrained enthusiasm for life with a new sympathy. Or the happiness she'd found in the town she returned to with such misgiving. Although a good part of the reason for that happiness was lying slick skin to slick skin above her, his chest heaving. "You're definitely worth waiting for . . ." she whispered, aglow with the utter sweetness of life.

"I'm lockin' you up," Billy gasped. Giving her a quick kiss, he rolled on his back, still breathing hard, wondering how the hell he could climax like that and still be alive.

Lily always had that lurching moment of jealousy and doubt when he was lying eyes closed and breathing like that after making love. He was too expert and too perfect and she always thought of the other million women who'd seen him like this . . . toned and buff, practically godlike in his beauty. He liked to call himself a small-town boy, but he had the women of the world after him, along with plenty of small-town women too. And with that unhappy thought, Heather's face appeared like an apparition from hell.

Calm, calm . . . take a deep breath. He doesn't care about Heather—he said so.

But suddenly, as if she'd lost her mind completely, she heard herself say, "You're not going to see Heather again, right?"

"Huh?"

Was that a yes or no, a question or a grunt? Even as she warned herself not to be stupid, she turned on her side so she could see his face. "Heather," she said.

Wrenched back from his really fine thoughts, Billy looked at her, clearly bewildered.

"I shouldn't ask. I'm sorry."

"Ask what?"

"I was wondering when you had to go back to work," she said, like someone whose brain was functioning once again.

"Oh." He shrugged. "I don't know." He smiled and reached for her. "Fuck work. I don't want to talk about work. I want to talk about keeping you here in bed with me for a thousand years."

"Only a thousand?" She was definitely getting addicted and smarter by the minute.

"Okay, a million," he said with a grin, "but you're going to wear me out."

CHAPTER 30

Billy came back to Lily's with her and met her guest. One look and Billy knew Tom Schaumberg's reasons for coming to visit hadn't been benign. But Tom took his defeat with good grace, and over a breakfast Billy had delivered from the Lodge, they found congenial ground for conversation. Tom was a hockey fan; he had season tickets for the Chicago Blackhawks. He'd played some himself in college. But when breakfast was over, he said, "I think I'll head over to Giant's Ridge now. That way I'll get in a day of practice before my competition arrives."

Good choice, Billy thought, but he only smiled. "It helps to go over the course before the tournament. They've put in another eighteen holes this year. It's a pretty fair course." He had his arm around the back of Lily's chair; they were seated across from Tom. "Thanks for taking care of Lily's divorce. She needed some first-class counsel, I hear."

"My pleasure," Tom said, thinking the star of the NHL worked fast. Lily had just arrived in town. But then he had a reputation with the ladies.

"Give my regards to Ben when you get back to Chicago," Lily said. "Tell him I'm settling in well."

"He'll be pleased to hear it." She looked happy. Brock wouldn't like to hear it. He was a possessive bastard.

"Who's Ben?" Billy asked.

"My partner." Apparently Brock wasn't alone in his possessiveness.

"They saved my property from Brock." Lily smiled. "I was *very* grateful."

And Tom had come up to Ely to collect his reward, Billy thought. "Then I'll add my thanks as well." Billy dipped his head toward Tom and smiled pleasantly because Tom was leaving. "It's really great having Lily back in town."

At lunch that afternoon, the air of contentment was flagrant. Even Ceci was willing to admit that she was currently in a romantic state of mind—a condition she had hitherto viewed as mythical or fictional.

"I actually wait to see Nick. *Him*—not him for sex, but *him*. Maybe angels can dance on the head of a pin after all," she said with a benevolent smile for the world at large, her friends in particular, and her memories of last night with Zuber.

"I told Frankie I love him," Serena said softly. "I've never told anyone that before and now I feel like . . . all spiritual and warm inside."

Ceci held up her hand as though warding off evil spirits. "I didn't say love . . . that's a couple decades off."

"How do you know? You never even thought about romance before. And look how you feel about that now," Serena countered. "Maybe you love Nick and don't even know it."

"I *loved* the absolutely fabulous sex I had this morning," Lily said with a grin.

Ceci gave her a knowing glance. "Billy got rid of your company?"

"I went to Billy's place. We talked to Tom when we returned."

"Did the guy notice you were still flushed from fucking?"

Lily's cheeks turned pink.

"Like that," Ceci said, grinning.

"How strange that Tom arrived without calling," Serena noted. "He should have given you some warning."

"Maybe he didn't want to take the chance of being refused. Is he good-looking? Did he turn you on?" Ceci asked.

Serena frowned. "Everything isn't about sex, Ceci."

"I don't think this guy drove to Ely looking for a walleye taco."

"Billy thought that too," Lily murmured. "It's possible, though Tom really had some lag time before the golf tournament."

Ceci snorted. "You're such a baby, Juju. So did he turn you on?"

"No! I mean . . . wasn't even thinking about that. Tom was the perfect gentleman."

"Unlike most men around here who consider sex a personal right if there's a woman with a pulse nearby."

Serena directed a puzzled look at Ceci. "I thought you weren't bitter anymore."

"That's not bitter. That's a fact." She smiled. "Nick promised to be good."

Lily's brows rose. "Is that a mutual agreement?"

Ceci shrugged. "He didn't ask."

"So, are you?"

"I haven't thought about it. This voodoo romance thing is taking up all the space in my brain right now."

"Frankie and I are going to live one day at a time." Serena hugged herself. "Isn't that romantic? It makes me all tingly. I'm bringing him home for dinner tonight which makes me all double tingly. I mean, it's just like in a movie."

"He didn't mind about Luke, then," Ceci said, caution in her voice.

"He was just a darling about it. He's so mature. But you know, in his job, he has to deal with real life-and-death situations all the time—so one little indiscretion wouldn't bother him. Or I suppose it wasn't really an indiscretion since we don't have an understanding or anything and I can go out with whomever I want—Frankie said that. Isn't he just impossibly adult about just everything?" she finished, beaming.

"Unlike Zuber who will be perennially immature," Ceci noted. "Not that I'm in the mood to complain at the moment. He's a hot, hot, burning-hot passion right now and I like the feeling."

"Do you ever think about getting married?"

Ceci shook her head. "Not me."

"Me either," Lily said. "I tried that once already."

"I wonder if Frankie ever thinks of getting married?"

"Remember, you've only known him a few days, Serena." Ceci was speaking in her extra polite voice that she used with her clients who wanted to do their entire house in pink. "You should probably wait before you spring that on him. Although dinner at your parents' house might be a clue."

"Frankie knows my mom and dad already."

"Then he won't be alarmed."

"Are you saying all men are alarmed about the thought of marriage? They can't be. Lily was married. She said she was coaxed into getting married. So there. Some men want to be married."

"And some men want to be married and still have girlfriends," Lily said.

"Oh, dear, I'm sorry, but you're not really mad anymore, are you? Now that you have Billy."

"I don't *have* Billy."

"You sort of do. I mean he's always over or looking for you or calling you."

"You've got him, Juju," Ceci said with a smile. "He just doesn't know it yet."

"Cyndi Lauper and I just want to have fun though." Lily grinned. "I don't want to *have* anyone."

"Except when you want him. For sex."

"You shouldn't talk that way," Serena protested.

"You were the lady who made a habit of cultivating rich old men with good taste in jewelry, darling."

"Well, I'm not anymore. I might even stay in Ely."

There was a moment of profound silence. Ceci and Lily were speechless.

"Is that so strange?" Serena's blue gaze was accusatory.

They had been good friends since grade school. This wasn't the time for the truth.

"Not at all," Ceci said.

"We could do yoga together," Lily said.

Ceci's cell phone rang and her face lit up when she answered it.

"Yeah. Yeah." A small frown began to crease her forehead. "I understand. Sure I understand, don't I sound like I understand? For how long? Uh-huh. Right. Look, don't ask me again. I'm fine. Really, I'm fine." She flipped the phone closed and scowled at her friends. "He's lying to me."

Lily kept her voice neutral. "What happened?"

"Zuber can't come over tonight. His sister's in town. I didn't even know he had a sister."

Lily nodded. "He does. His sister was about six or seven when we left. My parents used to golf with Zuber's folks. He's not lying about that part."

"Thanks for the vote of confidence."

"I didn't mean . . . I'm not implying he's lying— I mean . . . oh, shit . . ." Her voice trailed off.

"I'll ask my mother about his sister," Serena said. "She knows everything that goes on in town."

"How did he sound?" Lily asked.

Ceci blew out a breath. "He sounded harried."

"There. He's not lying. In *When Your Lover Is Lying*, disc two, right near the end of the CD . . . if a man's lying, he always goes on and on and on with his explanation when you never even asked." Lily had read every self-help book on the subject when she found out about Brock.

"Call Buffy." Ceci handed her phone to Serena. "It's not too early for a drink, is it?" Without waiting for an answer, she waved for the waitress and then leaned forward in her chair, her gaze on Serena as she dialed. Catching herself almost instantly, she muttered, "Fuck if I'm going to carry on like an idiot woman," and sat back.

"It's okay to be jealous," Lily said. "It's natural."

Ceci grimaced. "A margarita with Patrón silver on the rocks, no salt," she said to the waitress who had come up.

Ceci and Lily both turned to listen to Serena's conversation.

"Mummie, not *that* Zuber family. They're from Aurora. The Zuber family from Ely. How many children did they have? Uh-huh. We know that. He always wins those contests, Mummie—yes, the one climbing the lumberjack pole every Fourth of July too. But does he have a sister? Uh-huh."

Ceci's drink came and she drank half of it in one swig. "Men are jealous too," she said, as if she needed justification. Ceci had always prided herself on living her life like a man . . . take what you want, no hard feelings, it was fun while it lasted. She wasn't prepared for feeling affection and, worse, jealousy.

"Of course they are," Lily agreed. "It's perfectly natural," she said again, as though she was soothing a panicked child who had just discovered the world wasn't always like Barney said.

"She's been having what? Oh, I see. And she doesn't want to go home? No, Mummie, I just heard some gossip about Nick's sister and didn't know if it was true. I'll ask Lily and Ceci, but they might have plans. I don't know if they can change them, Mummie. I know everyone likes tenderloin, Mummie, but they still might have plans. I'll be home in time. Yes. Yes. Don't worry. Good-bye, Mummie. I have to go." She handed the phone back to Ceci. "His sister has been in and out of rehab. She's twenty now and not getting along with her parents. Her name's Desiree. Mummie says she's very nice, but sensitive and high-strung. She hit Principal Humbolt in the face once with her notebook."

"Shit. I should have been nicer to Nick."

"You can call and apologize," Lily said.

Ceci looked at her blankly.

"Apologize. People do that, you know."

"To men?"

Lily smiled. "Occasionally."

"I'll think about it."

"Mummie said to invite you both to dinner tonight. You don't have to come."

"Billy's making plans, but thanks."

"Thanks, but I'm going to check out this apologizing thing and wait for Nick."

"I'm going to wear my new lavender organdy," Serena said, with that faraway, life-is-a-rainbow look in her eye that had become familiar since Frankie had entered her life. "It makes me feel like Scarlett O'Hara." Which was appropriate when your mother was a relocated Southern belle. "Everything's going to be just perfect tonight!"

CHAPTER 31

That evening, Frankie came to dinner, Ceci apologized for the first time in her life, and Lily spent an evening that would be placed in her book of memories on the page devoted to sublime happiness.

Everything changed a little bit that night, as though there were levels of enchantment, and everyone took a giant leap toward paradise.

It started with Ceci because she was the most impatient.

As soon as she left the restaurant, she called Zuber.

"I'm sorry I was rude to you," she said, surprised by how easily the words fell from one's lips when one was overcome by romantic sentiment. "I know a good therapist for your sister. Should I see if she'll make a house call?"

Even though his brusque "Would you?" didn't impart a great range of emotion, she sensed that he was relieved.

"And just in case your sister is feeling better after she talks to Lucille, I'll leave that figurative light on for you tonight."

"Thanks. I'll come over if I can. I had to cancel my schedule this week so I'll be around."

Many of Ceci's friends in California had been in and out of rehab. She'd listened to all their dysfunctional suffering enough times to have a fair idea of the stages of therapy. And Lucille owed her about ten favors for doing her crazy Hollywood producer cousin's house without killing his blonde bimbo third wife in the process. That woman had changed her mind more often than George Clooney changed girlfriends. Although with better results. George Clooney was still looking, while Barbra now had a house that had been on the cover of *Architectural Digest*.

"Lucille, Ceci Cignoli here. I need a favor."

She called Zuber back to tell him that Lucille was on her way. She heard something break in the background and understood when he said, "Thanks, gotta go." Hanging up, she felt a warm glow like the one Serena was talking about. She had been able to help Nick. Not as she helped her clients, but rather as a truly sensitive, unselfish act of compassion.

Which just went to show you how curiously romance could impact one's life. Perhaps she wasn't quite ready to wear those floaty dresses and large-brimmed hats with long streamers, nor could she picture herself lying in bed in some lacy Victoria's Secret lingerie with a bowl of white roses scenting the air as she waited for her man. But she *was* willing to wait for Nick. And that, she recognized, was a significant first.

Walking out on the porch, she sat in her favorite wicker chair, reached for her notebook on the nearby table, and began writing about this new, enlightened universal goodwill and generosity of spirit.

Dinner at the Howards' went well. Frankie was on his best behavior, Serena spoke in effusive phrases, Buffy wasn't shorted on her martinis, and George Howard was by nature an agreeable man. Serena had to help Frankie with the sixteen pieces of silverware bordering his plate. He also wasn't used to a different wine with each course, although he manfully kept up—which earned him high marks from Buffy, who liked anyone who could match her liquor consumption, and respect from George, who didn't often see anyone walk away from the dinner table sober.

Coffee and dessert were served in the conservatory overlooking the pool, the baked Alaska offering a showy climax to the meal.

Not a discouraging word was spoken all evening.

The Howards were known for their hospitality.

"You were just perfect," Serena cooed much later

that night as she lay in Frankie's hammock with him. She was trying to decide if she'd like a Vera Wang bridal gown or one by Carolina Herrera, although she was careful not to mention it just yet. "Mummie said you were such a gentleman," she said instead.

"Thanks." He smiled into the starlit sky, knowing he'd been under scrutiny, but not much caring, doing it for Serena. "I've always liked your parents."

"Are you going to introduce me to your family?"

His breathing stilled. There was a moment of silence. "Sure, if you want."

"That doesn't sound very friendly."

He pulled her closer. "How about this weekend? Everyone's coming over for my mom's birthday."

"Really! I'd love to." Her mind was racing with possible birthday gifts. "How old will your mother be?"

He shook his head. "I'm not sure."

"What's your mother's favorite color?"

"Color?" he said as if she'd asked him the formula for the speed of light or the best trajectory for the rocket to Mars.

"Does she like bibelots?"

"Does she like what?"

It looked as though she was on her own. She'd get something tasteful, but modestly priced so as not to embarrass any of his family. "Don't worry, darling," she murmured, reaching up to kiss his cheek. "I'll get something nice."

He wasn't worried about Serena picking out a gift; he was worried about his outspoken family saying something outrageous to her. He'd give them all fair warning. If they fucked with her, he'd kill them.

"Thank you for inviting me," she whispered, snuggling closer.

This probably wasn't the moment to point out to her that she'd invited herself. "You're welcome, honey." He mentally crossed his fingers. "Everyone's going to love you."

Billy had come to pick up Lily at six, carrying a large bouquet.

"How lovely! White iris!"

"Is that what they are? Bonnie at the flower shop said they're locally grown so you can smell them without inhaling a dozen pesticides," he said with the male disregard for sentiment. "Or was it herbicides."

"Thank you and thank Bonnie." Lily took the flowers from him and walked into the kitchen to get a vase.

"She wants to see your garden sometime," he said, following her. "I told her you were planting all kinds of exotic things."

"Tell her to give me a call."

"Will do." He sat at the table. "Are you hungry?"

She turned from the sink. "Are you cooking?"

He shook his head. "Gracie is. I told her I wanted something special tonight for our anniversary."

"What anniversary?"

He grinned. "Our so-many-days-after-we-met anniversary."

"I hope you didn't tell her that." But her heart was thumping hard.

"Nah." He'd told her to pull out all the stops because he was crazy about Lily. Gracie had looked at him kind of funny. "The '24 Margaux crazy?" When he'd nodded, she'd grinned from ear to ear because she'd been telling him that when it hits, it hits, and he'd never believed her.

Not that he was admitting anything was hitting anything.

He'd been thinking about drinking the '24 Margaux anyway.

"You look great," he said, because Lily did and he didn't want to think about the reason for Gracie's silly grin.

She batted her lashes at him over her shoulder. "This old thing?" She was wearing a short, sleeveless linen dress in pale yellow, the back dipping in a deep vee to her waist where a tailored bow invited a hand to untie it. She was really turning him on.

"I bet they liked that on your TV show." She'd told him about her wardrobe. "Or at least all the men in the Chicago area did." He glanced at the clock, decided Gracie would have his balls if her dinner went cold, and came to his feet. "We probably should go."

Lily lifted the clear glass vase from the sink, the white iris arranged in what appeared to be an artless, graceful display.

"Zen," he said, admiring the purity of color and line.

She smiled. "I wish. It's my this-is-the-only-vase-I-have arrangement."

When they arrived at their table in the Lodge dining room, there were more flowers. Purple and white pansies in a low silver bowl.

Lily looked up at Billy. "This is beginning to feel like an occasion."

The table was separated from the other diners by a painted screen depicting a northern landscape. It was primitive in style, like so many of the furnishings that had been created by local talent over the decades the Lodge had been in existence.

Tom's visit had made him nervous, but he didn't say that. In addition, their disagreement over Heather had lost him a night of her company. Although their reconciliation this morning had more than made up for that loss. "It's a little occasion, I suppose," he said, pulling out her chair. "We're great together."

She smiled at him as she sat, each day etched in her memory.

"Definitely time for a celebration," he said, taking his seat opposite her.

The waitress materialized as if she'd been hovering in the wings, and took their drink order.

"Shaved ice," Billy repeated as she turned to go, and Lily felt as if she was a princess in a fairy tale, pampered and indulged by a handsome prince.

She sat back, clasped her hands in her lap, and

blew out a small breath. "I'm freaking out here. Someone's going to have to pinch me."

"Don't freak out until Gracie serves dinner. Otherwise, she'll crucify me."

"You can be a little overwhelming."

"Not compared to you," he said, smiling. "You're on my mind, twenty-four seven."

"So this is a mutual obsession."

"You'll see when Gracie comes. She's going to embarrass me, guaranteed."

"That's a relief. I mean . . . I wouldn't want to be throwing myself at you if you weren't ready to catch me."

"I'm more ready than you'll ever know," he said in a husky whisper. "In fact, I'm thinking this might have been a bad idea, because I want to carry you to bed right now, and—"

"You're going to have to wait on that," Gracie said with a smile, coming around the screen with a tray of hors d'oeuvres.

"Feel free to speak up, Gracie," Billy muttered.

"I always do—just to make sure you don't get a big head." She set the tray on the table. "These big-time athletes, you know." She grinned at Lily. "They need to keep their feet on the ground." Gracie was small and slender, her dark hair was in braids; she looked about thirteen. "You must be Lily." She held out her hand. "Gracie Gregorich. He's crazy about you, I hear."

"Do you mind?" Billy said.

"Just thought she'd like to know, since you're

probably not going to come right out and tell her. Although this"—she waved at the table—"might give her a clue."

"You're fired," he said, punching a finger in her direction.

"Can't fire me. I have a five-year contract."

"I'll talk to my lawyer in the morning."

"Does that mean you still want the meal tonight?" She was grinning broadly.

"You're lucky you're so good."

"You're lucky you're so rich or I wouldn't be here."

"Prima donnas," Billy said, smiling as Gracie took her leave. "It's the price you pay."

"How did you find her?" Lily surveyed the array of delicate hors d'oeuvres. "She's an absolute artist."

"Her husband came north and opened a photography studio. She needed a job."

"You didn't say she was married."

He smiled. "You didn't ask."

She wrinkled her nose at him. "Don't be annoying."

"Not me. I do everything you ask."

She thought for a moment and then grinned. "You do, don't you?"

He winked. "I'll show you just as soon as we're out of here."

CHAPTER **32**

It was almost midnight when Zuber called Ceci. "My sister's finally sleeping," he said, sighing deeply. "She's been crying for hours. If you want to come over I'll wait for you at the end of the drive. If you don't want to, I'll understand. It's really late."

"No problem. I was hoping you'd call."

"Leave your car at the turnoff. I don't want the lights or the noise to wake her up." He sounded exhausted.

"I'll be there in twenty minutes."

Zuber's cabin was a sculptural creation he'd built a piece at a time, the rambling structure following the contours of the rocky point he'd chosen on the lake. He was waiting midway between the cabin and the end of the drive, quickly approaching Ceci as she came into sight. "I don't dare go too far away. Des wakes up with nightmares when she's coming off drugs." He took Ceci's hand. "Watch your footing," he murmured, leading her toward the cabin.

He put his finger to his lips as they approached the door, then leaned close to her ear. "Sorry about the melodrama, but she doesn't sleep well."

Ceci nodded her understanding, then tiptoed behind Zuber as he moved into the house.

He led the way to his bedroom, walking without making a sound. Ceci tried to replicate his quiet tread, unsuccessfully. They reached his room without discovery, however, after which he carefully shut the door, pulled her into his arms, and kissed her long and hard.

"Jesus, I missed you," he murmured as his mouth lifted from hers. "It seemed like the longest day of my life."

She'd also experienced a novel sense of missing someone, but regardless of her new insight into love, the habits of a lifetime weren't so easily jettisoned. "I'm glad you called," she simply said. "Really glad," she added with a degree less temperance, beginning to unbutton his shirt.

"Not as glad as I am that Des finally went to sleep." He grinned. "You're my reward."

"And you're mine," Ceci murmured, sliding his shirt over his broad shoulders.

They undressed each other swiftly, each of them feeling the urgency, the need for quiet only adding to the odd feeling of illicitness. Their sexual relationship had always been more open than most, bereft of tranquility, unreserved. "I feel like high school," Nick whispered, sliding Ceci's slacks down her hips. "And my parents are downstairs."

"My sister's bedroom was next to mine and she was a tattletale. Now, there's pressure," Ceci whispered back, laughter in her eyes.

"You can't scream."

"I don't scream."

"Okaaay," he murmured, shifting to plan B in his head, lifting her by the waist and setting her very, very gently in the middle of his bed. He followed her down with equal caution, listening for mattress squeaks. He should have known, but he'd never been presented with this particular dilemma before. In the semiwilderness of his five lakeshore acres, it had never been an issue.

"Are you going to be able to—" Ceci's whisper ended in a suffocated gasp as Zuber slid inside her and her question was answered in a most delectable way, his invasion slow, slow, exquisitely slow, so they both felt the heat.

She clung to his shoulders in the darkness, experiencing an overwhelming sense of being engulfed by Nick's power and size—the sensation tremulous, fiercely intoxicating, as though she was indeed his reward and he was taking what was his. Perhaps the need for constraint provoked her arcane sensations of submission. It undeniably incited a ravenous desire and she rose into his downstroke, wanting more.

He tightened his grip on her hips and gave her what she wanted, what they both wanted.

The heights were higher, the flame hotter that

night. Perhaps their senses were more overwrought or maybe their hearts were involved. Whatever the reason for their orgasmic bliss, Zuber had to muffle Ceci's screams, covering her mouth with his so many times that she finally noticed.

"Sorry," she breathed.

"Don't be sorry. You two look good together."

Ceci's eyes flew open and she stared in shock at the figure standing in the doorway.

Zuber quickly moved off Ceci and jerked the sheet up to cover their nakedness. "Get out, Des."

She didn't stir. "Aren't you going to introduce me?"

He rolled over on his back and slowly exhaled. "Ceci, meet my sister, Des. Des, this is Ceci. Now get the hell out."

"That's not very friendly. You're nicer to Ceci, I hope. Do you like my brother, Ceci? Most women do . . . actually all women do, don't they, Nick?"

"I'd really appreciate it if you'd go back to your room, Des." His voice was mild, like the voice you'd use to keep someone from jumping off a bridge.

"He always talks to me like that so I won't start crying again. Nick hates it when I cry, don't you, Nick?"

"How did you like Lucille?" Ceci asked.

Zuber shot a glance at Ceci, his brow creased.

Des shrugged. "She's not as bad as some of them. Is she your shrink?"

"Not yet. Depends on how long I know your brother, I suppose."

"No shit. This whole family is fucked."

"Thanks," Zuber muttered.

"Hard to find a family that isn't these days." Ceci grinned. "Too much violence on TV."

"Not enough prayer in the schools."

"And women aren't walking two steps behind men anymore. Culture is in disastrous decline," Ceci said with a smile.

"Hear that, Nick? You men are on your way out."

"You better hope I'm not or you won't have any-place to crash."

"You have a point. He has a point," Des said, nodding at Ceci.

"Sometimes men are useful," Ceci noted.

"Most of the time they're not."

"If you two ladies are going to gang up on me, I'll get my ass out of here and go get a beer." Wrapping the sheet around his waist, Nick rose from the bed.

"Bring me one back." Ceci looked at Nick's sister. "You're on the wagon, I suspect."

"I have to."

"Good girl. Make ours Cokes, Nick."

When Zuber came back into the bedroom, the women were sitting cross-legged on the bed, comparing therapists. And by the time he'd drunk his beer and Ceci and Des had drunk their Cokes, the two women were like long-lost friends. He didn't stop to think that a woman who struck an emotional chord with him might do so with his sister as well. But then he didn't think about emotional chords; in fact, he made a point of not thinking about emotion at all.

It was a long-standing habit of his.

He saw it as a matter of survival.

CHAPTER **33**

The two men met at the Evanston Country Club bar.

Tom Schaumberg pulled out a bar stool and sat down. "How was your round of golf?"

"Seventy-four. Nothing special. You?" Brock Westland smiled his practiced smile.

"A lousy eighty-one. I couldn't buy a putt."

The bartender took Tom's order.

"I saw your ex a couple of weeks ago," Tom said, watching his companion with a trial lawyer's scrutiny.

Brock was expressionless. "Here in the city?"

Tom shook his head. "In Ely. I was playing in a golf tournament up there."

A flash of agitation transiently illuminated

Brock's eyes. "Did you go out with her?" The men had been adversaries over the divorce, but it hadn't affected their nominal friendship or usefulness to each other. Business was business.

"I was thinking about it. But she's spoken for," Tom drawled, enjoying Brock's discomfort.

"What the hell does that mean?"

"She's sleeping with someone. From the looks of it, on a regular basis."

"How do you know?"

"He shared breakfast with us."

"I get the feeling you're going to tell me who he is," Brock said with silky sarcasm.

"Billy Bianchich."

There was no mistaking the fury in Brock's eyes. "It didn't take her long."

"Longer than you," Tom pointed out, his voice mild.

"Screw you."

Tom took his drink from the bartender and lifted it to Brock. "Just thought you might like to know."

The bland mask was restored to Brock's face. "It's none of my concern who she fucks."

"True. Bianchich seemed real involved though. I was surprised. He has a reputation for sleeping around. He didn't seem like the kind of guy to settle for one woman. Is Sherry still keeping you interested?"

Brock shrugged. "She's hot enough." He lifted

one perfectly trimmed brow. "And it never hurts to have a coanchor who's not out to knife you in the back."

Don't be too sure, Tom thought, but he was capable of bland smiles too. "Sounds like a plan." He drained his single malt and stood. "Next time," he said.

Brock watched him walk away, his scowl pronounced. It was obvious the bastard was baiting him. Brock pushed his drink away. On the other hand, this might be the perfect time to do a short piece on the Boundary Waters. With summer vacations in full swing and the dog days of newscasting leaving plenty of room for fillers, it could turn out to be a serendipitous opportunity.

He came to his feet. He'd run the idea past his producers. If they approved, he'd have his researcher put together a dossier on the great Billy Bianchich before he left. An eye opener, as it were, for sweet, naïve Lily.

CHAPTER **34**

The next few days were an idyll of happiness, pure and simple. Billy moved some of his things into Lily's cabin because she was busy in her garden and didn't want to live at his place. Ceci spent more time at Zuber's than at home, her ability to connect with Desiree a win-win situation for them all. Serena asked Frankie if he'd mind if she did a little decorating at his cabin and his tactful enthusiasm was keeping her busy moving fabric swatches from room to room.

Even Heather had taken a hiatus from her pursuit—something to do with poison ivy.

Saturday morning dawned with a golden glory that presaged another perfect summer day—the possible awkwardness of the pancake breakfast notwithstanding.

When they woke that morning, Lily made a last attempt to renege. "My lady's slippers are looking unhappy. Maybe I should stay home and see if I can put up something to shade them."

"Coward," Billy said. "I'll build you some shade trellises when we get back."

"You will?"

"Yep." He knew what worked with Lily, other than sex, of course. Anything to do with her plants.

She sighed. "I suppose I'll go."

"You already said you would."

"I'm trying to avoid hand-to-hand combat. I'm not good at it."

Billy grinned. "I won't let Heather touch you."

"Promise?"

"I already promised you ten times. You're like a little kid."

"I hate confrontations. I avoid them like the plague."

He wanted to say that avoiding Heather in a town this size was impossible. Hell, avoiding Heather when she was on a roll would be impossible in Manhattan at rush hour. "There won't be any confrontations," he said instead, lying through his teeth. "I promise."

But Lily took a very long time finding something to wear that morning. She changed three times, couldn't decide on her shoes or perfume or jewelry and was, in general, so dilatory, Billy finally stood in the bedroom doorway and said, "If you're not dressed in five minutes, I'm taking you in your underwear."

She'd always had nightmares about appearing in public in her underwear.

Heather's eyebrows rose clear into her hairline when Billy walked in with Lily. She'd saved a seat next to herself at the table and had actually risen to her feet and begun waving when he appeared in the doorway of the Community Center dining room, only to stop, arm raised, openmouthed, when Lily appeared beside him.

Her gasp alerted her mother and Mrs. Bianchich. They both looked up. Ethel frowned, quickly caught herself, and restructured her expression. Billy's mother didn't bother to conceal her shock, nor her delight. Billy must be interested in Peggy Kallio's daughter if he was bringing her to a family affair like this. It was about time he found someone he liked.

Mr. Bianchich and Markie returned with their plates of pancakes just as Billy and Lily arrived at the table. The ensuing remarks concerning pancakes and Eddie Halprin's time-honored recipe that was always used at the hockey breakfasts eased the stilted moment.

On the other hand, that period of superficial conversation also gave Heather time to load her guns. "Billy, I saved you a seat by Markie," she said, pulling out the chair beside her, pointing her son into the chair on the other side of the empty one. "You don't mind, do you, Millie?" she said, looking directly at Lily with a saccharine smile. "Markie and Billy are such *good* friends."

The resemblance between Billy and the boy always disconcerted Lily, not that she would have known how to respond to such blatant rudeness anyway.

Marlene Bianchich, in contrast, knew exactly what to say. "Harold, pull over another chair for Lily. Put it right there." She waved in the direction of the empty chair. "Sit beside Billy, dear," she said, smiling at Lily. "Harold, you remember Jim Kallio's girl. She's two years younger than our Alicia. Your mother used to bring you over to play with Alicia, but you were only two or three then." She had Billy's eyes and they were friendly. "I don't expect you remember."

"Alicia was on the swim team with me."

"Of course. You swam in the relays together. Billy, have you forgotten your manners? Get Lily some pancakes. Harold, give your pancakes to Heather and then bring some back for Ethel. I'll get mine later. I like the ones from the bottom of the batter. They're thicker."

A general couldn't have deployed her troops better.

The ladies were left at the table, along with Markie, but he was busy eating and unaware of the petulance hovering in the air like a police helicopter in South L.A.

Ethel trained her gaze on Lily. "Will you be staying in town long?"

You couldn't accuse her of beating around the bush. "I have a year's contract to teach at the community college," Lily replied, resisting the urge to run.

Ethel's lips firmed. "I see." If it had been a movie, the kettle drums would have begun an ominous rhythm. "And then where will you go after *that*?"

Lily was tempted to say, "I'm planning to go to the slums of Calcutta where I'm sure to contract some lethal disease that will take my life in under forty-eight hours," just to see Heather and her mother smile. "I'm not sure," she said instead.

"Excuse me," Heather said, jumping to her feet as though she'd been struck by a bolt of lightning. "I need some more coffee." And she made straight for Billy, who was standing in the pancake line.

"Heather and Billy have known each other since they were children," Ethel said, smiling at her daughter who was practically glued to Billy's chest and looking up at him with an adoring gaze.

Her usual pose with him, Lily thought, wondering what in the world he'd seen in her. Heather arched her back at that precise moment, thrust her large breasts into Billy's chest, and Lily was reminded of the T-shirt she'd seen in a catalogue emblazoned with the words:

TEN THINGS MEN KNOW ABOUT WOMEN.

One through nine were blank and number 10 read,

WOMEN HAVE BIG BOOBS.

So much for male replies to the question, What are you looking for in a woman? The usual answers—a sense of humor, intelligence, fun to be with—were gross misrepresentations. Heather's 36 Ds were what they were looking for.

"You must tell me about your garden. Myrtle Carlson has been spying," Marlene said pleasantly. "I hear you've really changed the shoreline for the better."

Dragging her gaze away from the demonstration of the T-shirt axiom, Lily tried to shift her thought processes away from the words *conniving bitch*. "I'm trying some new hybrids that hopefully will survive the winter. You're welcome to come see my garden. You too, Mrs. Drollet," Lily offered, not because she wanted to, but because courtesy required it.

Ethel gave Lily a withering look. "Flowers make me sneeze."

"I adore flowers," Billy's mother said. "You'll have to give me some advice on my garden."

"Heather grows the most beautiful roses," Ethel lied. Her daughter's roses were the result of liberal doses of Miracle-Gro she personally dispensed. "Heather would be more than happy to give you some tips."

Before it became an outright Challenge of the Garden Titans, Billy and his father returned with pancakes, Heather in their wake. The plates were passed to the appropriate people, everyone took their seats, at which point Heather pulled her chair as close to Billy as humanly possible and leaned into his arm. "Do you think Markie should try to play goalie?" she asked with a breathiness more appropriate to the last stages of intercourse.

Billy leaned away. "If Markie wants to try, talk to Curt on Monday."

"I'd really like it if *you'd* help him."

"I don't play goalie. Curt knows that position better."

"But he just *adores* you," she said, shifting to a little-girl voice that may have been charming ten years ago, in dim light even seven years ago. "Don't you, Markie?"

Markie heard his name and looked up. "Huh?"

"Darling, tell Coach Bianchich what you said to me about him last night."

Markie's blank look wasn't a deterrent to his mother.

"He said you were the nicest coach he'd ever had, didn't you, darling." She smiled sweetly at her son who had gone back to his eating. "He's such a lonely little boy now that . . . well"—she sighed—"his father never sees him. Your camp has just been a godsend for him this summer." With impeccable timing, tears appeared in her eyes.

If Markie didn't bear such a strong resemblance to Billy, Lily would have been able to blow off Heather's wet-eyed seduction, but the nagging suspicion remained. Was Billy capable of ignoring his own son? Did Heather have good reason to pursue him?

Lily lapsed into a troubled introspection, the words *conniving bitch* replaced with the unfortunate phrase *mother of my child*—the disturbing thought almost impossible to ignore with Markie's little face two feet away.

As Marlene deftly turned the conversation to the ice arena's budgetary goals, Lily only half-listened, sunk as she was in her slough of jealousy and suspicion.

When the Hockey Association president rose to make a few remarks about the children and parents' enthusiastic participation in the program, Heather took the opportunity to direct warm smiles of understanding Billy's way as though they were some of the parents alluded to.

Billy was praying hard that Joe Horton wouldn't speak long because he could only take Heather in small doses and Lily looked as if she was in a trance. He didn't know whether to be grateful or alarmed at the zoned-out smile on Lily's face, but the minute Joe finished thanking everyone for their volunteer work, Billy jumped to his feet. "It was great to see you all," he said, pulling Lily's chair back, almost bodily lifting her up, "but we have to go. I promised to make some trellises for Lily's garden."

With her ordeal over, Lily's smile was genuine for the first time since they arrived.

As they exited the room, Billy took her hand in

his. "I shouldn't have asked you to come. Heather's a major bitch."

"Is Markie your son?" So much for frontal-lobe censorship and tact.

Dead silence greeted her query for a disconcertingly long moment.

"Is that what you think?"

Answering a question with a question was Evasion 101. "Is he?" Lily persisted, almost completely bereft of inner poise after watching smug Heather in action.

"No."

"Just no?"

"Is there another way to say it?"

"He certainly *looks* like you."

"Everyone on the Range looks like me. Black hair, dark eyes, only size and gender differ. Italy or Yugoslavia, that's mostly it for ethnic background up here."

Along with a few Finns who liked to live back in the bush where no one could tell them what to do and the Cornishmen who'd come to run the mines. "I *know* what people look like here, but Heather seems to be suggesting there's more to your relationship."

Billy exhaled a long, slow breath. "Even if she is, it's not true."

His answers were too vague—like Brock's. "Make me believe you," she said.

Billy's nostrils flared and a muscle twitched over his classic, Greek-god-type cheekbones that she shouldn't be noticing at a time like this when she was very near losing her temper.

"I don't have to make you believe anything. He's not my son. Period."

"He could be." She should let this go. She should be hip enough to understand that past relationships had nothing to do with her. Did Cleopatra care that Julius Caesar wasn't a virgin when she was unrolled from that rug at his feet, so long as she had his attention?

"Look, I haven't seen Heather *that* way for nine years. Okay? The kid's six. And don't look at me like that because I can't help what she says. Once I left town after high school, I never saw her again. Believe me or not, it's the truth and you're starting to piss me off."

"I wouldn't want to do *that*."

Billy pulled her to a stop outside the Community Center. "Let's not fight over this. It's stupid. Heather's a manipulative bitch and I feel sorry for her kid. So if I'm nice to him, that's why. No other reason. Okay?" He bent low, so their eyes were level. *"Okay?"*

Trust was a loaded word. Uncertain and contrary. But however suspicious she'd become because of Brock, deep down she still believed in the goodness of the world. And Billy's eyes were clear of guile and so beautiful—along with the rest of him—that she'd be ten kinds of a fool to censure his past. "Okay," she said with a sigh.

"Damn, you make me happy." He kissed her

right there in front of all the people who were beginning to walk out of the hockey breakfast, and then he swung her up into his arms, said, "Let them look," and kissed her again.

Even though she believed in the goodness of the world, and nominally in turning the other cheek, and of course, intellectually in Zen spiritual forgiveness, Lily couldn't help but hope with the tiniest bit of malice that Heather was watching.

CHAPTER 35

The backyard of the Aronsons' farmhouse was shaded by large maples under which several tables ladened with food were set. A keg of beer, wrapped in an old quilt, was ensconced in ice in a galvanized laundry tub on legs. The yard was filled with cars, people and children, dogs and cats. Serena had never seen so many dogs and cats in one place. Or so many children. It was bedlam, but she didn't say that of course. She said, "How wonderful to have such a large, extended family."

"Sometimes," Frankie said, surveying the crowd. "Sometimes they're just a pain in the ass."

Someone waved.

Frankie waved back.

A piercing wolf call rang out and every man,

woman, and child, along with several of the ani-
mals, turned to look at them.

"I guess they've seen us," Frankie murmured,
the charged silence palpable.

Serena slipped her hand into Frankie's. "Why is
everyone so quiet?"

Because they've never met a millionaire's
daughter before. "Who knows," he lied. "Come on,
I'll introduce you."

While Frankie warded off a friendly assault
from various dogs, they walked toward a group of
women seated on lawn chairs. As they approached,
a tall, slender, gray-haired woman dressed in
magenta-colored slacks and a white blouse rose to
meet them. She was smiling.

"Mom, I'd like you to meet Serena Howard.
Serena, this is my mom."

Flo Aronson put out her hand. "It's so nice to
meet you." She grinned at her son. "I've been hear-
ing stories."

"*Mom!*"

"Good ones, Frankie. She's cute."

Blushing, Serena shook Frankie's mother's hand
and handed her the package she was carrying.
"Happy birthday from us."

The *us* brought Flo's gaze back to Frankie.

He ignored the speculation in her glance. "I told
her she didn't have to."

"I wanted to, Mrs. Aronson."

"Flo."

"Flo. I hope you like it."

"I'll love whatever you brought, sweetheart. Frankie, go and get Serena some food. I'll introduce her to the girls."

The girls were all over-eighty aunts from both sides of the family who never missed a party. They'd all lived in Ely forever and knew stories and gossip that went way back, like the time when the music teacher ran away with one of his pupils or when the mayor was caught with his pants down literally, or when Uncle Joe ate so many pancakes at the church breakfast that his record still hadn't been broken. Everyone had a story, and before long Serena was feeling all cozy and warm in the bosom of the family—like in the old show *The Waltons*, only not so poor, of course, and no one wore those drab clothes.

When one of the aunts put her great-granddaughter in Serena's lap and the darling little baby girl looked up at Serena and cooed, "Mama," for the first time in her life she felt a rush of maternal tenderness. She'd never even felt a twinge of benevolence toward children before; she'd scarcely noticed them. What would Frankie and her baby look like? she wondered, smiling at the chubby baby in her arms. He'd have to have Frankie's curly black hair and dark eyes—the first one would be a boy, of course, because she'd always wanted an older brother. She'd dress him in the sweetest little baby clothes from those sweet little shops in New York that had motorcycle jackets for three-month-old babies and little tennis shoes that fit into the palm of your hand, or sometimes in those soft French baby clothes that had little embroidered teddy bears on the Peter Pan collars. And they'd come to picnics like this and their babies—because they'd have a girl too—would join the children racing across the lawn just like in those ads for Windstar vans and Chevy Suburbans.

Although she liked the Mercedes station wagons too. She'd have to talk to Frankie about that. She supposed if she was married to a county sheriff, she probably shouldn't be riding around in a Mercedes because then they'd begin to investigate him and everything—like they always did on *Dateline* when some government official in some remote county in Texas or Tennessee looked too rich. She'd have to talk to her daddy about that. Although maybe he drove a Buick for a reason.

Frankie's hand on her arm brought her back from her reverie. "If you're done eating, I'll introduce you to the rest of the family."

After the tenth sister or brother-in-law, Serena didn't even try to remember names. There were fifty-eight all told of the Aronson clan. Frankie kept his arm around her shoulder—a blatantly protective gesture his brothers and sisters recognized—as they did the warning glances he gave them over Serena's head if any of them looked as if they might step out of line. For a family known for their pranks and candor, in Serena's presence they all behaved like angels. Although Frankie took the precaution of leaving right after the birthday cake was served.

By that point, the keg was almost half gone and there was no relying on anyone's behavior.

"You look just like your father," Serena said as they were driving back into town. "He seems very nice. Everyone was so friendly and pleasant."

"Good. That's good." Frankie was just starting to relax now that they were five miles down the road, although he kept glancing in the rearview mirror. His brothers had the habit of trying to run each other off the road in a playful game of chicken. With pasture on both sides of the road it was a benign enough sport and he never was the one who ended up in the hayfield anyway, but Frankie didn't know how Serena would view such antics.

He turned left at the crossroad, taking the long way home. Just in case.

"Have you ever thought about another use for that little room at the back of your cabin?" Serena suddenly asked, babies occupying her thoughts almost exclusively. She could just see herself in a floaty dress with a ribbon in her hair, sitting in a rocking chair decorated with painted pictures of nursery-rhyme characters, holding an adorable sleeping baby in her arms. "You just have old fishing tackle and junk in there now."

"What do you have in mind?"

"Don't be frightened."

"Okaaaayyy," he said warily.

"Someday, it could make the sweetest nursery."

"A nursery?" he croaked. He cleared his throat and smiled at her. "That's an idea . . ."

"Really? You wouldn't mind—I mean . . . really and truly? You're not just humoring me?"

"Someday, sure, I'd like kids."

"Don't say it like that, like someday—with someone . . . maybe," Serena said, her bottom lip going all pouty.

He took a deep breath. "I'd like a baby with you," he said, his voice without its usual volume. "Really." He didn't want to fight; it wasn't going to happen anyway because she'd be gone soon. There were times when you just said the words to keep everything in balance.

Serena threw her arms around his neck and left a trail of kisses on his cheek. "Should we do it tonight?" she whispered, snuggling closer.

The phrase, heart-stopping, was no longer a rhetorical question. For a second, Frankie wasn't sure he could catch his breath.

"Please, please, *please*," she purred. "Can we make a baby . . ."

CHAPTER **36**

WHAT DO YOU MEAN THEY DON'T
HAVE OUR RESERVATION! TELL THEM
WHO I AM, FOR CHRISSAKE! FUCKING ID-
IOT! DID YOU TELL THEM WHO I AM?" Brock
was seated in a rented SUV parked outside the
Lodge, the passenger side window down, perspira-
tion beading his forehead, trickling down his neck
to the collar of his Italian shirt.

"Yes . . . yes . . . I told them—I did," the trembling young man stammered, red-faced, sweating
profusely after running back and forth between the
desk clerk and his boss because Brock didn't seem
to understand English. "The clerk insists he doesn't
have any record of the reservation. It's the weekend
of the Blueberry Festival," Kevin Dunlop said as if
to a five-year-old—very slowly because Brock had

apparently missed the point. "And the Lodge is booked solid. He suggested the Super 8; his aunt or cousin or someone said they might have some rooms."

It took Brock a moment to put his horror into words. "I'm going to pretend you didn't say that. If you can't find me something better than a Super 8, fuckhead, you're out of a job. Is that clear?"

"Yes. sir—yes . . . absolutely." Although after eight hours of travel with the Brock, Kevin wasn't sure being canned would be all that bad. They'd taken a flight to Minneapolis that Saturday morning, then one to Hibbing, where they'd rented cars for the drive to Ely. If those eight hours hadn't been hell, they'd been a harrowing practice run. "I'll make a few calls," he said, backing away as one did in the presence of royalty.

"Chip-chop, Yalie turd," Brock growled, taking his cigar case out of the inside pocket of his custom-tailored straw-colored linen sport jacket and drawing out one of his Cubans. "Why me?" he muttered, clipping the tip of his cigar. "Why do I get all the incompetents?" Lighting the smuggled Cuban with his Dunhill cigar lighter, he leaned back in the seat, blew out a stream of smoke, and surveyed the view: the neat green-shuttered cabins dotting the lakeshore, the blue lake visible to the right and left of the main lodge, the fishermen in their boats at the docks.

With his thoughts on Lily, however, the picturesque landscape was barely registering on his retinas—not that landscape ever much did anyway. Was she fucking her young stud right now? Were they working up a sweat in the sack? Was the glory boy athlete ramming his cock into her tight little cunt this very second? Brock's eyes narrowed against the smoke, his mouth firmed in a grim line. Who would have thought little naïve Miss Backwoods would be making it with the wunderkind cocksman of the NHL. Maybe he should have paid more attention to her when they were married. Maybe she was more X-rated than he thought. His mouth curved into a nasty smile. He'd go have a look-see for himself just as soon as his stupid assistant straightened out their lodging. Maybe he'd have a little taste of his ex-wife before he left town—see what she'd learned from the Boy with the Golden Cock.

It should be interesting, handing Lily the dossier he'd collected. It was always gratifying to shine the spotlight on scandal. He expected she'd be surprised at the broad scope of Mr. Billy Bianchich's conquests. Hell, he was surprised. He smiled. Investigative reporting had such a wonderful capacity to ruin lives.

Kevin leaped down the entrance stairs and ran to the open window of the car. "There was a cancellation at the conference center in town," he gasped. "You have a room."

"It's about time." Brock jerked his head in the direction of the driver's seat. "Get in and drive me there."

It turned out the rest of the crew would be housed at the Super 8. A matter of necessity with only one cancellation, although Kevin, for one, didn't mind the physical distance between himself and Dickhead as Brock was fondly referred to by those at WCGO who had to take his orders.

"You and the crew scout out locations and have my script ready by tomorrow morning," Brock instructed as they drove toward town. "The usual summer getaway scenes. There's some wolf center here that people get all jacked up about, and do something about the fishing and canoeing thing, I suppose. Hell, I don't care. Just make sure I don't have to talk to any of the locals. If you want local flavor, do it in voice-overs. Bring me my coffee and usual breakfast at eleven sharp. Three-minute eggs, not a second more. And I better have a lake view," he warned. "Did you bring my monogrammed sheets?"

Within the hour, Brock's monogrammed sheets had been put on the bed in his lake-view room, the hotel manager was having a stiff drink in his office, the desk clerk was patting cold water on her tear-reddened eyes, Kevin was lighting up a Brock-relieving Bob Marley spliff in his Super 8 room, the camera crew was scouting locations in the nearest bar, and Brock was parked in the SUV outside Lily's cabin—in a high state of frustration.

She wasn't home.

There was evidence of her presence—her gardening gloves and sundry pots of flowers were on the porch steps, a half-drunk can of Coke had been still cool on the railing.

Should he stay and wait for her return or drive into town looking for her? He tapped his fingers on the steering wheel and scowled. Dammit! Where the hell was she? He'd been looking forward to seeing her expression when he showed her the list of women Billy Bianchich had gone through in his five years in the NHL. He was also looking forward to seeing his new sexpot ex. Shit. Where was she?

As if on cue, a red Ace Hardware truck came up the drive.

Brock frowned.

She was with *him*. Bianchich's face was unmistakable—from the sports pages and TV, from the tabloids.

Jesus. People usually looked smaller in real life than on TV—but not Bianchich. Maybe he'd show Lily the dossier later.

Lily recognized the full-set-of-white-teeth camera smile almost before she recognized her ex-husband. "What's he doing here?" she murmured, watching Brock stroll toward her.

Billy caught the disdain in her voice and looked more closely at the tall, blonde man. "You know him?"

"That's my ex and he doesn't like Ely or the outdoors. I can feel the hair rise on the back of my neck because he's a long way from the bright lights of Chicago."

"Want me to send him on his way?" Billy's voice was mild.

Lily glanced at Billy's narrowed gaze. "No, I don't want you to send him on his way if that means what I think it means. I'll deal with him. You stay here." She smiled. "Sorry, I forgot you boys paddle your own canoes up here. But be polite, will you?"

"It depends."

"This isn't a challenge match."

"I know that."

"You don't look like you know that."

"How do I look?" Billy smiled his own full-teeth smile. "Is that polite enough?"

Lily laughed. "I don't believe this is happening in the twenty-first century. I feel I should be swooning or giving my scarf to you to pin on your sleeve before you go off to save me from the dragon."

"Cute." But his opponents on the ice would have recognized the ominous look in Billy's eyes. "What the hell is he here for?"

"Good question," Lily said, opening her door. "Promise you won't make trouble."

"I never make trouble," said the man whose fighting abilities were an asset on his NHL résumé.

"You're a long way from home," Lily said as she walked toward Brock. "Did you make a wrong turn at Sherry's driveway?"

"You blew that way out of proportion." Brock

shrugged away his infidelity with a lift of his shoulder, the soft linen of his jacket rippling gently. "The station sent me up to do a vacation-in-the-north-woods spot. They say go and I go. You know me."

She did and he only went where he wanted to go or all hell broke loose and anyone within range of his anger paid dearly. "What can I do for you?"

"I just thought I'd stop by and say a friendly hello."

She didn't offer him a friendly hello in return. "Are you going to be in town long?" she said instead.

"A couple of days. I'm Brock Westland." He put his hand out to Billy who was standing beside Lily, towering over her, actually. "Nice town you have here."

"Billy Bianchich. Thanks, we like it."

Brock wasn't a small man but Billy's hand dwarfed his.

A small silence fell.

"Good luck with your vacation piece," Lily said, breaking the silence. "If you'll excuse us, we're doing some planting."

"The garden looks good. But then your garden always did."

"You never noticed. Or if you did, you said, 'How's your girlie garden doing,' if you recall. Goodbye, Brock." Lily walked away; Billy met Brock's gaze for a potent moment, and then followed her.

And Brock Westland, who was not only used to but required deference and major ass-kissing, was left standing in the drive.

CHAPTER 37

He's not very big."

"Nobody's very big compared to you. Is he gone?" Lily was walking toward the shady part of the yard where her lady's slippers were having a trellis constructed for them.

"He's going. That's one smooth-looking, tailored-to-his-fingertips guy."

"Do I detect a question in that remark?"

"It's none of my business."

She smiled up at him. "You got that right."

"Does he wear silk underwear?"

"I'm assuming that's a facetious question with that grin on your face. It wouldn't be a serious question since the state of his"—she'd never liked Brock's name; it sounded like a candy bar—"underwear falls into that none-of-your-business category."

Billy jabbed his finger at her and grinned some more. "I knew it."

"Monogrammed yet."

"No shit." His voice took on a new gravity. "So what the hell did you see in him? No offense."

"I don't want to talk about it."

"Fine. No, really. Tell me. You don't even like him. It shows."

"Are you my therapist?"

"No. Although after seeing him," he said, smiling broadly, "the thought occurred to me that you might need one."

She punched him. "Don't talk to me about therapists after Heather."

"I was young."

"Last Tuesday night?"

He grimaced. "I blame my mother."

"See . . . it's not always so easy to say no."

"You couldn't say no to marriage? I think I could manage that."

"And you probably have unless I miss my guess."

"You don't want to know."

"And you don't want to know the illogical and witless reasons that made me say yes to marriage." She punched him hard this time.

He knew when to drop a discussion—when her jaw was twitching like that. He smiled. "You don't hit very hard. Is that the best you can do?"

"Watch out or I'll beat you into submission."

"You just have to crook your little finger for that, babe."

"And you'll do anything?"

He pulled her to a stop. "Anything at all," he said softly. "You just name it."

She glanced at her lady's slippers. "We *could* do the trellis later. They wouldn't mind."

"That's what I heard too," he whispered just before he kissed her.

They ignored the ringing phone a half hour later, and when it rang for what seemed forever an hour after that, they still ignored it. But the third time the caller from hell started on the twentieth ring, they were lying contented in the bed and if they had been smokers they would have been sharing a cigarette about now.

Billy nodded at the phone. "Want me to get it?"

"I'd say yes if not for the fact it might be one of my relatives or someone from the college or one of my mother's friends wondering if I want to come for dinner—like all of them seem to be doing—or Myrtle next door who calls on any—"

Billy rolled his eyes, reached for the phone, and handed it to her.

"It's you," Lily said, frowning, and the identity of "you" was immediately apparent. "No. No, I don't want to." Her frown deepened and Billy slid up to a seated position. "Yes, I'm sure. That means, yes, I'm sure I don't want to." She slowly exhaled. "That's really no concern of yours." Her face flushed bright pink. "You're way out of line, there. I'll be hanging up now." She tensed and tears sprang to her eyes. "Why didn't you say that? Of course I want it." She glanced at the bedside clock, gave Billy a quick smile, and took a deep breath. "I'll be there in twenty minutes. In the lobby," she said firmly, and handed the phone back to Billy to hang up.

"Do you need a ride?" Billy asked, although it took effort to keep his voice level.

"Yes, I do."

He felt relief wash over him; he didn't like the feeling. "What was that all about?" he asked, hostility in his voice.

"Don't you give me shit too."

"Too?" He couldn't get a handle on his tone.

"Yeah, too." After she'd listened to Brock's snide remarks, her temper was up. "I don't need a man questioning my life."

He put his palms up. "Fine." The last thing he wanted was some woman hassling him. He understood. "Where're we going?"

"The convention center on Shagawa Lake. He has my grandmother's picture. Don't ask me how he has it, but I want it back."

There was no need to ask to whom she was referring. "I'll be ready in five," Billy said, swinging his legs over the side of the bed.

When they reached the center, Billy pulled up to the entrance and smiled at her.

"I'd ask you to come in, but—"

"You don't want to."

She grimaced. "I guess. He's such an ass. I won't be long."

Brock was seated on a couch near the massive stone fireplace in the lobby. As she approached him, he patted the seat beside him.

"Just give me the picture. I'm not interested in visiting."

"I saw your boyfriend drive you up."

"Good for you."

"Do you know what they call him on the hockey circuit?"

"A good player? The picture, Brock, if you please. I don't want to talk to you."

"I don't have the picture, but I have something else you might like to see." He lifted the file folder in his lap and handed it to her.

"You bastard. I should have known. You and the truth don't even have the same zip code. Whatever you have, I'm not interested in."

"Just take a peek. It's about your boyfriend."

"He's not my boyfriend. You have boyfriends in high school."

"Did you know he's slept with—" Brock's smile was oily. "You probably should count them yourself. There's pictures too. Interesting pictures."

"Who the hell are you blackmailing? Shouldn't you be talking to him?"

"I'm just *concerned* about you."

"Right. I'm going to need boots pretty soon."

But she hadn't walked away, he noticed, so Brock

went for the jugular. "Billy boy's had three paternity suits brought against him. Did you know that?"

She told herself his past didn't matter. She told herself that groupies went with fame. She tried to ignore the fact that a man who made his own decisions existed beneath the celebrity. And failed.

"You can take this with you if you like." Brock lifted the file folder again. "I've another copy."

She took it from him. "You're still a bastard, aren't you."

"Maybe I'm not the only bastard in your life, honey." He nodded at the folder. "Take a look at some of those fascinating pics."

She turned to go and then swiveled back. "Don't call me again. Not on any pretext. If you do, I'll hang up."

He leaned back and looked her up and down. "Now why the hell would I want to call you?"

"We agree then. Good." And if it had been a movie instead of real life, she would have slapped him hard before she left and said something cryptic about getting even. As it was, she walked to the ladies' rest room, entered a stall, locked the door, and leaning against the wall, her heart beating like a drum, began thumbing through the contents of the folder.

"Holy shit," she kept saying, until someone in the next stall called out, "You okay in there?"

"I'm fine," she said, her voice resonating in her ears as though through a mile-long tunnel. But she was careful after that to utter her expletives under her breath as she flipped through the photos and clippings, the sinking feeling in the pit of her stomach worsening with each revelation.

Once she'd seen them all, she closed the folder and opened the stall door, hoping no one was around. A young girl at the sink glanced over her shoulder. "Are you going to be all right?"

Lily glanced at herself in the mirror, saw she was ashen. She lifted the folder. "Job stuff," she lied. "My boss is trouble."

"You can sue him." The girl grinned. "Ain't it great?"

Lily was pleased to see that she could smile. "That's an idea." She began moving toward the door.

The girl held up her fist. "Go get 'im."

From the mouth of babes, Lily thought as she walked down the corridor. The young girl couldn't have been more than seventeen. She pinched some color into her cheeks, reminded herself she was strong, independent, as capable of attitude as a seventeen-year-old. As for Brock, she hoped never to have anything to do with him again. And as for Billy, worldly and open-minded as she was—it would take considerable open-mindedness to overlook *that* number of women. When the hell did he have time to play hockey?

After she got back into the truck, she handed Billy the folder. "Brock had this for me, not my grandmother's picture." And then she watched him.

He was expressionless as he flipped through the

contents. Then he closed the folder and handed it back to her. "Why did he give this to you?"

"That's it? Nothing about you?"

"There's quite a bit about me in there. But what's it to him—as if I didn't know? He still wants to hurt you."

"And you don't?"

"Some of that stuff isn't true, but I'm not going to give you a bunch of excuses. Some of it is true. But I didn't know you then."

"Don't you think this . . . this . . . excess reflects on you to some degree?"

"I just don't say no all the time. But believe it or not, I say no *most* of the time. I prefer playing hockey to all this shit."

"I'm not feeling good about these pictures to begin with and you're taking this way too casually."

He exhaled slowly. "Do you want me to go through each one of those and tell you whether I slept with the woman or not? Some of those pictures and articles are tabloid fodder; they're not true."

"Why not sue them then?"

"I don't care enough to bother. I know who I am. Do you want an apology? Is that what you want?"

She looked away, feeling exhausted—as though she'd not slept in days. "I don't know what I want."

"That ex of yours is good at jerking your chain. I'll give him that. Fucker."

It was never a man's fault, was it? How did they

manage to go through life without accepting any responsibility? "Would you take me home?"

He started to say something, changed his mind, and shoved the gearshift into first.

No one spoke on the ride, resentment palpable.

What the hell did he have to be resentful of? Lily thought. Resentment was her exclusive territory on this issue.

She got out without a word.

"Don't forget your folder," he said curtly.

"Keep it for your scrapbook," she snapped.

CHAPTER 38

This is a going-down-for-the-third-time emergency," Lily said into the phone. "No excuses," she added, interrupting Ceci.

Serena was helping her mother sort through her old letters and file them by year, so she responded to Lily's request with enthusiasm, and promised to bring over a box of Godiva truffles.

But ten minutes later, three women, not two, arrived at Lily's.

"Lily, Desiree Zuber, Desiree, Lily Kallio. Desiree doesn't want to be alone right now," Ceci said with a significant look for Lily. "So we came together. And she has boyfriend trouble too. Join the club, right?"

"Men are bastards," Lily said. "Or maybe just the men I know. Does anyone want a drink?"

"We're not drinking," Ceci said. "Cokes are fine."

"A glass of some white summer wine sounds nice," Serena said.

"The mood I'm in, I'm chugalugging a fifth of brandy."

"You don't even drink brandy," Serena said, wide-eyed.

"Brock's in town."

"I know a man who'll solve your Brock problem. All it takes is a phone call," Ceci said. "No, I mean it. Really."

"I wish," Lily said. "But then I'd get my name in the paper and my parents would be embarrassed."

"It's all very discreet. No names. No papers. Just two broken knees and Brock's on his way back to Chicago in an ambulance."

Serena frowned. "Ceci, don't talk that way. I'm sure this situation with Brock can be solved in a more civilized way."

"Poison in his pâté?"

"Who's Brock?" Desiree asked.

"Lily's ex. One of the world's first-class jerks."

Desiree cocked one brow at Lily. "And you married him—because . . . ?"

"Because Lily was naïve, she's incredibly sweet, she thinks that the whole world speaks the truth, and Brock wanted something he couldn't have."

Desiree grinned. "You could write advisories for George W. Keep it short."

"I didn't get the impression your crisis had to do with Brock, though," Ceci said with a rare tenderness.

Lily shook her head and tears came to her eyes.

"I'll get the wine," Serena said, jumping up.

"Have my Almond Joy," Desiree said, pulling the bar out of her shirt pocket. "What? Doesn't everyone eat Almond Joys?"

"I do, thanks," Lily said, taking it from her. She unwrapped the bar and shoved half of it into her mouth.

Ceci gave her a knowing look. "It's about Heather, right?"

Lily shook her head again, still chewing. "It's more like fifty Heathers," she mumbled.

"Wait until I get there!" Serena screamed from the kitchen. "I don't want to miss anything!"

Once Lily and Serena's wine was poured, and Desiree produced a second Almond Joy for Lily to go with the box of truffles, once Ceci had found two Cokes and everyone was in place, Lily began her account.

"Where's the folder?" Ceci asked when she'd finished. "I don't believe Brock for an effing second. He probably doctored the photos. With computers, you can put anyone with the president if you want—hell, you could put him with Castro in his bath."

"Billy has the folder. And I don't think the pictures were doctored."

"But you don't *know*," Serena said. "I saw a photo of Russell Crowe with Margaret Thatcher in some tabloid. How weird is that? And if I saw some photos of Frankie with someone I didn't want to see him with, I'd give him a chance to explain. Did you ask Billy about them?"

"Not really."

Ceci scowled. "I would have knocked him on his ass, sat on his face, and made him explain."

"If you were sitting on his face, he couldn't talk," Serena pointed out.

"It was an expression, kitten. I'd want an explanation if for no other reason than to watch him squirm."

"After all those pictures and clippings I wasn't in the mood to watch him squirm or listen to what would probably be a bunch of damned lies." Lily grimaced. "I just wasn't up to it."

"After Brock, I don't blame you. He makes you think the whole world is tainted."

"I've never seen so many gorgeous women, though," Lily said with a sigh.

"Sometimes those ladies are just looking for a photo op with a celebrity," Ceci noted. "Maybe you should let Billy explain."

"He didn't seem real concerned with explanations. It was like, that all happened before I met you—never mind. I wonder if he'd care if I had a gajillion lovers in my bedroom Hall of Fame scrapbook—no offense, Ceci."

"No offense taken, sweetie. I've always enjoyed the ride differently than you. By the way, I'm on my second scrapbook."

"Nick and Ceci are soul mates," Desiree said, grinning. "They both think pleasure makes the world go round. I'm trying to learn the same attitude."

"And I'm trying to tell her everyone's different. And that's okay."

"Diversity, right?"

"Exactly. Lily, Serena, and I have been friends for-ever and we all have a very different worldview. But it doesn't matter. Just like it doesn't matter that your boyfriend didn't turn out to be the one for you."

"I know what you mean," Lily agreed. "Although Billy apparently has been the one for every *other* woman this side of the Mississippi."

"Don't be bitter." Serena leaned over and offered Lily the box of truffles again. "You just wait and see. There'll be some perfectly rational explanation for all those silly pictures."

"With his looks and fame, there's always going to be women," Lily noted. "I don't care to listen to end-less explanations or, worse, nonexplanations." She took a bite of a mocha truffle. "It would be too an-noying."

"You *do* have a quick temper," Ceci remarked, her tone tactful in view of Lily's misery.

"I didn't say anything terrible, if that's what you're thinking."

"You did say he was mad."

"For no good reason, if you ask me."

"Maybe he'll apologize," Serena offered.

"That won't solve anything. Don't you see—with his in-the-limelight sports career, there'll just be an-other folder and then another one after that. I'm go-ing to cut my losses now before I get in too deeply. I just need you all to listen to me whine until I'm sick of the sound of my voice or I pass out or both." Lily saw the quick look pass between Serena and Ceci. "I don't mean it literally. You're excused anytime."

"Frankie gets off work at five and well . . . we *were* going to dinner at his brother's, but I can call and cancel."

"No, don't do that. I'll be fine."

"We can stay till six," Ceci said, "if that's okay. Or later," she quickly added at the look on Lily's face. "Really . . . our schedules are free."

Lily almost said, "You have to stay," because both Serena and Ceci were happy and she was dismal, but she couldn't be so selfish. "Six is great. Is that bottle of wine almost empty? I'll get another. Serena, you're not drinking." She jumped up and ran into the kitchen to hide her rush of self-pitying tears. Wiping her eyes on the kitchen towel a moment later, she gave thanks to all the bacchanalian gods for grapes and chocolate, pulled another bottle of wine from the fridge, and returned to the living room.

But neither wine nor chocolate were enough once her friends were off to their happy, merry, blissful relationships and she was left desolate, alone—and angry. She felt like strangling Brock with her bare hands, but that would be an instance of too little too late, now that all those photos of movie-starlet types were floating through her brain. And Brock was just the messenger, after all, although, let's face it, he was one nasty son of a bitch. Not that she cared to dwell on the fact that he was an SOB, because that made her the world's most gullible woman—or perhaps the second most gullible after Monica, who thought Bill was going to marry her someday.

It was amazing what a woman would believe—more amazing what a man would say to get laid. Or in her instance, get married. She'd never quite understood what had prompted Brock to pursue her to the point of marriage. Ceci's pithy "she was something he couldn't have" seemed too trite. A shame she hadn't been able to detect the deceit beneath Brock's charm.

Now, of course, sadder and wiser, every word Brock spoke was judged by her built-in fraud-finder. But, Brock aside, the reality of all those photos and clippings was devastating. She gazed at the lone truffle in the box, decided there was no point in counting calories once you were past the magic six thousand mark, and in the depths of gloom, she needed solace. She picked up the pecan-coated gooey chocolate sphere. So far today, she'd had pancakes, wine, and chocolate—which left her derelict in all the food groups that actually sustained human life.

But then chocolate fought tooth decay. She popped the truffle into her mouth.

"You know what picture I hated most?" she almost said aloud, catching herself just in time before she became one of those pathetic women who talked rambling nonsense to themselves after one or two—or at the most four . . . all right, five—glasses of wine.

"The one with Miss World—or was she Miss Sardinia or South London, whoever—hanging on Billy's arm as though she couldn't stand by herself on her five-inch stiletto heels with her huge breasts pulling her over," the voice inside her head answered . . . *not out loud.*

Lily immediately looked down and felt inadequate. Or maybe just cowardly. She could have just as big breasts if she had a higher threshold of pain.

Lily heard a phone ringing. At first, she thought it was the one on TV because she was half-watching the old Hitchcock movie with Jimmy Stewart in the wheelchair and Raymond Burr murdering his wife in the building across the street and Jimmy Stewart's phone kept ringing and ringing and ringing. Until Jimmy picked it up.

Strangely, the ringing in her ears didn't stop.

Her brain took several seconds to process that information and then she lunged for the phone, although in mid-lunge she hoped like hell it wasn't Brock, which just went to show how very well she could hold her liquor since she could still remember that concern. Although she might be just slightly inebriated, she decided as she and the phone fell off the couch onto the floor.

Several loud thumps, clangs, and startled expletives later, she said, "Hello," trying to sound casual.

"Are you okay?"

"I am now," said the uncensored tart living deep in her psyche who couldn't get enough of Billy Bianchich and overlooked all his numerous sins, half breathless with delight.

"I made a list. Ten yeses, nineteen nos. That wasn't so bad, I thought. Do you want to see it?"

She should say no. That definitely wasn't an abject

apology or even an apology. She should say, I never want to see your shockingly handsome face and studly body ever again. She should say, What list, because she didn't know what in hell he was talking about. "Bring over some food," she said, instead. "I'm hungry and I'm all alone because my friends deserted me when I really needed them—which just goes to show you that the only person you can count on is yourself." She sighed melodramatically. "You come into the world alone and you leave it alone."

"How much have you drunk?" Billy asked, instead of commenting on her philosophical observation on the state of the individual in an unfeeling society.

"A little wine," she answered, although she had trouble with the *ts*, and when she thought about correcting her pronunciation, she couldn't remember the question, so she said, "Food," with the intensity of a refugee from a boat lift gone wrong who hadn't eaten in ten days.

"I'll be right over," Billy said. "Don't move."

She didn't have any trouble complying because it felt much, much better to simply lie on the couch with the breeze blowing in through the windows Serena had opened "to waft away the reek of wine." Lily thought herself very clever to remember Serena's exact turn of phrase—so nineteenth century, actually, and perhaps etched on her memory because of its uniqueness. Speaking of which—uniqueness, that is—she wondered what kind of food Billy would bring over. Maybe some of

Gracie's wonderful hors d'oeuvres—those delicate little works of art like food sculptures—or maybe a huge slab of steak, which was particularly mouth-watering and appealing after so many chocolates. Had she mentioned how lovely the breeze from the lake was? she thought, apropos of nothing. So Miss What's-her-title had huge tits, she mused in her flitting state of mind that had nothing to do with the wine but was rather an indication of her superior ability to multitask. One could only feel sympathy toward the poor, poor dear beauty queen who would always look like a small mountain range when lying down. As for the lady's no doubt constant fear of toppling over when she stood, one could really only feel a deep, deep compassion.

So it really didn't matter that Miss What's-it had humongous breasts; *she* had lady's slippers. You see? It was all about balance. The cosmic world was about balance and diversity, give-and-take, ying and yang . . . all guided by a kindly spirit of dispassionate benevolence. What a nice term. So, well, benevolent . . . and serene . . . and calm.

She'd just rest her eyes for a moment before Billy and her food arrived.

Really, just a tiny, brief moment.

CHAPTER 39

Lily's house was quiet when Billy opened the kitchen door. Setting a box of food on the table, he moved toward the living room, warily.

Regardless of Lily's lack of hostility on the phone, she was obviously not exactly sober.

Reaching the living room, he came to a stop in the doorway, a smile forming on his mouth. Then he walked to where she lay sleeping, took a flowered throw from the back of the couch and covered her. After putting the food in the fridge, he took the damning folder he'd brought with him, placed it on the coffee table beside the couch, pulled out a single sheet of paper with two handwritten columns running down its length, and set that page on top of the folder.

He took a deep breath, swung his arms at his sides, blew out his breath.

If he were a praying man, this would have been the time.

Instead, he picked up the glasses scattered about the room, brought them into the kitchen, placed them in the sink, and walked out the kitchen door.

The sun was setting when Lily opened her eyes, although in summer, sunsets were late. Rising on one elbow, she squinted at the clock. Nine thirty-six. Digital clocks were so wonderfully precise; one never had to guess. Lying back down again, she suddenly remembered why she was alone and a rush of desolation flared through her mind.

As she gazed blankly at the ceiling, her peripheral vision took note of a folder lying on the coffee table. Since her subconscious viewed folders as repugnant, it took a brief interval of furiously tumbling brain synapses before she actually turned her head and looked at it.

Oh my God! He'd been here! Did she really want to look? Could she? Or was it better to continue in half-ignorance and denial?

That was his handwriting though—a swift, heavy script.

Could she ignore it? Or more to the point, how long could she ignore it?

A second later, she held the sheet of paper in her hand. A new record for lack of control.

One column was titled "Tabloid Fodder," the other, "Unfortunately True," and under each heading were listed women's names. She quickly counted the Unfortunately True list, then the Tabloid list. Ten and nineteen. Then she added up the number of men in her life to date—because she was deeply compassionate, not because she was influenced by Billy's sinfully handsome looks and well . . . superb physical, er, attributes. That would have been shallow and superficial. She then weighed the men in her life against the celebrity quotient of a sports superstar and began to feel somewhat better. If she could believe Billy's list, and she wasn't entirely sure she could, but *if* she could, he was—under the terms of her readjusted calculations—practically a monk. She chose to overlook the women who may have passed through his life without benefit of paparazzi documentation. But then the saying "love is blind" is a venerable, time-honored maxim not just recently coined for Lily, so if she chose to overlook a minor fact or two or ten, she wasn't completely alone in viewing the world through a conveniently skewed lens.

The grinding rasp of a circular saw shattered her increasingly compassionate thoughts, and unless Myrtle Carlson had gained a new skill since yesterday, she had a visitor. Throwing aside the light blanket, Lily jumped up and raced to the window.

Her darling Billy was building her trellises. How sweet.

She flew into her bedroom, looked in the mirror, and let out a strangled shriek. *He'd seen her like this.* Her mascara was smeared from crying, her eyes were puffy and red—same reason. His fault, but that was all in the past now with the equation of his and her love partners coming out not so very far apart after all.

Her hair was sticking out as if she'd been in a very strong wind, and why she'd decided to wear this disgusting old college T-shirt—even though it always brought her good luck, like now—was beyond comprehension. She must make a note to always fall asleep looking well groomed and fashionable, in the event handsome men who make love so incredibly well that there was a good reason for those starlets to be smiling might walk into her house unannounced.

Throwing off her faded T-shirt and shorts, she quickly rummaged through her closet for some suitably romantic, making-up-type outfit that wouldn't look out of place to a man who was pounding nails and sawing boards. A very difficult, specialized motif that rarely appeared on the pages of *Vogue* or *Elle,* she realized as she flipped through her wardrobe.

"Don't bother," a low male voice said. "I like you just the way you are."

"I'm not going to turn around until you get out and shut the door. My hair's a mess." She decided not to call attention to her smeared mascara, in the event he'd forgotten.

"You're the boss."

She always felt a shiver race up her spine when he said that in that low, husky tone that meant the exact opposite in sexual parlance. Her voice was trembling slightly when she said, "Go."

The sound of the door shutting galvanized her into action. In only ten minutes of quicksilver speed, she was once again presentable—face scrubbed, a light touch of mascara and lipstick applied, hair brushed, a sleeveless white piqué shirtwaist with buttons running down the front, just in case—her choice of making-up dress.

When she opened the door, he was leaning against the opposite wall, looking dramatically male.

"Nice," he said, his appreciative gaze traveling down her body and up again, coming to rest on her eyes. "If you don't mind my saying so."

That little hesitation in his voice was enormously appealing, along with that beautiful, direct gaze. She was surprised Brock could only come up with ten hits. "I don't mind. You look pretty good yourself." He was nude from the waist up, his rippling abs and delts gleaming with sweat, his jeans riding low on his lean hips.

"Aw, shucks, ma'am." He gave her a crooked grin and then held out his hand. "Your lady's slippers are happy. Come look."

She moved toward him, he pushed away from the wall, and their hands touched lightly before his fingers closed over hers.

"Thanks for the list," she said, smiling up at him.

"I thought it might help."

"I'm really sorry about Brock."

"It's not your fault. He's just a predator by nature. To hell with him, come see the trellises."

They were beautiful, arranged in a lovely zigzag pattern that shaded her plants and gave a charming dimension to that corner of her lawn. Billy had even stained them already—in the Prince Charles gray-green she'd had mixed at the hardware store that would weather beautifully, as the royal gardeners had probably already ascertained. Her lady's slippers were happy; she could tell.

And she was happy standing beside Billy, her hand in his, admiring her garden and his handiwork, at peace with her reservations and quibbles. Deep down happy.

"Thanks," she said. "For the trellises."

"You're welcome. Thanks for your understanding."

"I don't mean to frighten you, but I'm really happy. You may disregard that comment if you find it alarming."

"I'm not alarmed," he said, meaning it for the first time in his life after a woman confessed her feelings for him. "I'm happy too." He drew her into his arms and kissed her in the twilight, sweetly—a young boy's kiss. Then he raised his head and offered her a dazzling smile. "This is the real deal, isn't it?"

He was irresistible—a mixture of strength and innocence, toughness and sincerity, so handsome she always had to remind herself that looks weren't everything. Did he mean it? Was she willing to take a chance—with him . . . with his adoring fans? "It sure feels like the real deal," she found herself saying, suddenly not caring anymore about woulda, shoulda, coulda, wanting him now, right this minute now—*like Ceci, for God's sake.*

She must have eaten too much chocolate—the aphrodisiac enzymes were kicking in—although the way she was feeling right now was really not at all negative. It was glorious, like the feel of his body against hers was glorious. Hmmm . . . very, very— all her cognitive functions were zeroing in on the glory. Sliding her hands up his chest, she rubbed against him like a cat in heat.

Billy got the I-want-sex-right-now message loud and clear, and glancing out of the corner of his eye, he checked out Myrtle's place for lights. No lights. Coast clear. Cupping Lily's bottom in his palms, he dragged her into his erection. "You want it here? In that white dress?"

She grabbed his crotch and squeezed hard.

He growled and shoved her hand away. "Don't."

"What if I do?"

He hesitated for a moment, his gaze measuring. She stuck out her tongue. "You're not so tough."

"You sure about that?"

"Pretty sure." She moved back a step and lifted her skirt.

She wasn't wearing panties.

In a pulse beat, he was rock-hard. He began unzipping his jeans. "Come here." He said it low and smooth as butter, and then he kicked off his sandals, slid his jeans and underwear down his hips, stepped out of them, and the phrase "make one's mouth water" took on a new significance.

How many women had thought what she was thinking? How many times had he seen that look in a woman's eyes? She shook her head. "You come here."

She hadn't forgotten all those clippings.

She hadn't forgotten those clippings, he thought.

For a moment no one moved.

Then Billy walked toward her because when it came to sex, any judgment calls were pretty much made by his libido. "You win," he said, slowly forcing Lily back against the trellis.

"I know. You don't like to wait." She could feel the slats against her back, Billy's hard thighs pressed into hers.

He could have reminded her who couldn't wait the most, but he wasn't stupid. "Maybe next time," he said, pushing her dress up. Easing her thighs open with his palms, he flexed his legs and slid inside her with the finesse of considerable practice in bar hallways and bathrooms.

She was slick, wet, welcoming. He didn't want to think of how often she'd been like this with other men, flame-hot and willing—or how many men had done what he was doing to her. Maybe she knew about bar hallways too. She was already panting, meeting the rhythm of his strokes, clutching at him with a vengeance. Impelled by an inchoate jealousy, he drove upward with brute force, lifting her off her feet, burying himself hilt deep.

Proving who was stronger if nothing else.

She sighed, as though he'd given her the prize she'd always wanted and maybe he had. He was back. "I'm glad you came over," she murmured, no longer concerned with other women in his past when pleasure was melting into her pores. She was beyond the point of caring.

"You're mine," he said gruffly, tightening his hold on her, ignoring the incredible significance in such a remark.

"Yes, yes, yes . . ." Unspeakable pleasure coursed through her body; she would have said yes to anything.

He took a deep breath, oddly satisfied. Then he slid his hands under her bottom, hoisted her waist high, wrapped her legs around his hips, spread her thighs wider, and leaned into her, the trellis creaking as he forced himself deeper.

She started to climax. Quickly raising her as she whimpered, he muttered, "Wait," then he pressed her downward again, at the same time he rammed upward, hard. The shock hammered at her brain, sent waves of feverish sensation up her spine, down to her toes, curling through her vagina. "Don't move," she gasped, digging her nails into his shoulders. "Or I'll kill you."

Not that he could have stopped her orgasm if he'd tried, he thought, smiling, and seconds later, her scream echoed over the lake. When her breathing returned to a semblance of normal and her lashes lifted, he smiled at her. "Did I do good?"

"Oh, yeah." She licked a slow path across his cheek to his mouth. "Thanks, as usual, as always . . ."

His teeth gleamed perfect and white in the gathering darkness. "No problem, Miss Lily. The night's young."

"You mean you want to come too?"

"I was thinking about it," he said mildly, carrying her to a grassy plot near the lake.

She grinned. "You're way too cool."

"And you're one hot babe." He lay on his back and pulled her down on top of him.

Resting her arms on his chest, she smiled at him. "I love when you indulge me."

"Good. Because I like to." There was no explanation. Although, if there was, he was the last person to go looking for it.

Just feeling what he was feeling was enough.

They made love that night under the stars—playfully, tenderly—at times with a soul-stirring intensity that pushed the boundaries of fevered sensation. Until suddenly, the wind died down and

the mosquitoes came out—very inopportunely—
as they were nearing orgasm. Quickly rolling over
Lily, Billy covered her with his body without missing a stroke. She was making those little whimpering sounds she made near the last; this wasn't the
time to say, Wanna go inside? And stopping right
now wasn't high on his list of priorities either. In
the stage he was in, he couldn't have said *Mississippi* even once fast—or cared if he could.

A heartbeat later, Lily rose into his downstroke
and went still as her climax began—his cue to hit
the jackpot at the same time.

But postorgasmic moments later, the world returned and Billy became conscious of the cloud of
mosquitoes swarming over him. Swearing, he
grabbed Lily, lifted her into his arms, and bolted for
the cabin.

In the kitchen, Lily slapped away the remaining
mosquitoes, fretting and fussing at the number of
bites he'd gotten. "Oh, dear, oh, dear, oh, dear . . .
you were eaten alive. Let me run a hot bath for you
and get some lotion—you're going to need something for the itching," she murmured, turning
to go.

He caught her wrist and pulled her back. "Hey,
they're just mosquito bites. It's no big deal. Come
here," he whispered. "I'm not done with you
yet . . ."

CHAPTER 40

The next morning, Ceci called to see how Lily was.

"Perfect," she said, her voice redolent of good sex and white frosted cinnamon rolls from Gracie's kitchen.

"He's back."

"Sort of. He left for work."

"But he'll be back."

"Oh, yeah . . ."

"I can practically feel the waves of bliss from here."

"That's because he's pretty special. Mosquitoes don't even bother him, you know."

"Does that mean something cryptic?"

"I'll tell you later."

"Why not now?"

"Because he's on hold and saying really nice things to me."

"See you at the Chocolate Moose in an hour. I'll call Serena."

"Don't tell me, let me guess. You were talking to Lily," Zuber said, grinning as Billy approached the booth in Vertins.

"Yeah, so?"

"So everyone in the restaurant wished they could have heard what you were whispering out there on the sidewalk."

"How's your sister?" Billy asked, ignoring Zuber's comment.

"Bonding with Ceci. It's scary."

"And equally scary is the fact that Serena likes my family," Frankie noted.

Billy sat down and turned his coffee cup right side up for the waitress who had come over. "But outside of that, things are great, right?"

Frankie smiled. "Can't complain."

"Couldn't be better," Zuber said with a lift of his brows.

"Same here. I told Lily to plan a party."

"Any special reason?" Frankie asked.

Jolene stopped pouring coffee.

Nick put down his egg-ladened fork.

"No," Billy said, surveying the interested gazes. "I just feel like celebrating."

"Celebrating what?" Jolene asked.

"Life in general." Billy smiled. "If that's okay with you?"

"Just thought you might have an announcement," Jolene said. "You're not getting any younger."

"Is it possible to get some breakfast along with the advice?"

"Maybe, if you talk to me real nice."

"The usual. Was that nice enough, 'cause I'm hungry."

"THREE EGGS OVER EASY, HAM, WHOLE WHEAT TOAST, JUICE," Jolene shouted across the restaurant. Then she finished pouring Billy's coffee. "You did good this time, Billy. Don't let this one go," she said with a wink and walked away.

"Myrtle wasn't even home last night. How does everyone know?"

Frankie shrugged. "News travels like jungle drums. On the air."

"So where's this party?" Zuber asked.

"At Lily's tonight. She has fewer neighbors than I do at the Lodge. Bring your sister or anyone you want. Same with you, Frankie. I'm just in a damn fine mood."

Serena, Ceci, and Desiree were waiting for Lily when she glided into the Chocolate Moose. There was no other word for it when one was walking on air.

Ceci smiled at Lily as she sat down. "Things going your way again?"

"You might say that. Or you could say I've found the yellow brick road to paradise."

"Compliments of Billy Bianchich."

Lily smiled at her friends. "He seems to be involved somehow. We're having a party to celebrate our anniversary."

"What anniversary?"

"Billy said it was 10 days or 12 days or whatever since whatever." Lily fluttered her hands and grinned.

"Men *do* remember those occasions."

"But it's just a party. Tonight, at my cabin, if that's convenient for all of you?"

"I love parties," Serena said. "May we dress up?"

"Wear whatever you like. Gracie's cooking."

"Then I won't eat today. I want to have room."

"Who's Gracie?" Desiree asked.

"The chef from the Lodge. She worked with Pierre Gagnaire in Paris," Serena said with awe.

"And she's in Ely?"

"Her husband likes Ely. It helps that Billy pays her New York wages."

"Tell us every little detail," Ceci interrupted. "Did he apologize? How did he apologize? Did he call? Did you call? And I want to know what that remark about mosquitoes means." Ceci grinned. "Start with that."

A bright yellow moon hung in the starlit sky just slightly to the right of the island in Burntside Lake. The Slackers song about love gone wrong was vibrating through the open windows. The cabin was filled with people; a bartender from the Lodge had worked up a sweat keeping up with the crowd. Gracie was mingling, accepting compliments, her husband at her side. Desiree had found a friend of the Siminich brothers who had just gotten out of rehab and they were sharing war stories at the kitchen table. Everyone was enjoying the "good mood" celebration.

Serena and Frankie had wandered out onto the porch and were sitting on the swing. Not long afterward, Ceci and Zuber had come out to cool off from dancing and had taken a seat on the old metal glider. Billy and Lily strolled around the side of the house a short time later, hand in hand. Murmured greetings were exchanged as they joined their friends on the porch.

A balmy contentment underlay the squeak of the glider and the subdued rasp of the swing ropes; well-being pervaded the night.

"Great party," Zuber said.

"Really great," Frankie murmured.

Serena sighed. "Gracie's food was to die for."

"I think I'm in love with her," Ceci said. "Her crabmeat puffs are orgasmic."

Lily smiled. "It's the touch of fennel . . . an aphrodisiac, they say."

"It's working its magic," Ceci said, grinning at Zuber.

"Are we ready to go then?" Zuber drawled.

"We're trying to have a baby," Serena blurted out.

A proverbial pin-dropping silence fell.

The women stared at Serena, the men at Frankie. To say they were amazed would have been an understatement. Aghast was probably closer to the truth.

"Isn't it exciting?" Serena squeezed Frankie's hand. "We're so, so happy!"

Billy found his voice first. "Congratulations."

"*Trying* is the operative word," Frankie said, looking oddly constrained.

"But it's bound to happen!" Serena exclaimed.

"Wow," Ceci murmured, at a loss for words when she thought of Serena with a baby. "Wow."

Serena beamed. "I knew you'd be excited for us!"

"I'm really happy for you," Lily said, hoping her reservations didn't show. Serena and motherhood were like trying to make Ru Paul into Mother Teresa. Something of a miracle would be required.

"Hey, man, all the best," Zuber said, offering Frankie a thumbs-up. "Waddaya say, Ceci. Wanna make a baby?"

It was Ceci's turn to look constrained. "Not right now," she said with a tight smile.

Zuber grinned. "Say in about an hour?"

"Let's talk about this later."

"Since when did you become shy?"

Ceci's gaze narrowed.

"Later's good," Zuber said with a smile, relatively immune to censure in a life that had been, to date, one of transcendent good fortune.

"Nick, I'm going home with Christopher." Desiree stood in the doorway.

The glider squealed as Zuber jumped off. "Not till he's vetted by me, you're not. Where's the dude?"

Much later that night, having left the mess from the party for Billy's cabin at the Lodge, Lily and Billy were lying in his bed. The silk birch leaves overhead were shimmering in the breeze from the lake, the silvery moonlight poured in the windows, and all was right with the world.

"That talk of babies tonight makes you think, doesn't it?" Billy murmured.

Lily smiled up at him. "Not about babies, I hope."

He shrugged and grinned. "It's a thought."

"Hellooo . . . It's not a thought for me. Got it?"

"Roger that. But I was thinking, if this is going to turn serious, one of us is going to have to change their name. You know, 'Billy and Lily' is way too cute."

The word *serious* sent little shivers of happiness coursing through her already deliciously heated body. But this was still Billy Bianchich who was going off to training camp in a couple of weeks. "I've always liked the name Joe," she said lightly.

His grin was close, his body even closer, flesh against flesh, his weight braced on his elbows. "Would that be short for Josephine?"

She looked up into his amused gaze, but it was hard to smirk with your attention distracted by the hard length of a really magnificent erection nudging your vagina. "I thought you'd prefer Joseph," she purred. "Are we done talking?"

He softly laughed. "To be continued . . . In the meantime, happy anniversary."

It turned out to be the very best of anniversaries.

One of those all-night, etched-on-the-pleasure-centers-of-the-brain memories that made Lily seriously consider whether nirvana might not be just a spiritual state of mind.

Less prone to searching for the meaning in life, Billy gave voice to his happiness the next morning in a more prosaic way. "Okay," he said. "You might be able to talk me into Joe."

"You're so sweet," she said, running her hand down his hard, muscled arm that was harder and more muscled than any arm she'd ever seen, a thought that sent delicious little ripples fluttering deep inside her because he was so wonderfully hard and muscled *everywhere*.

She sighed.

Sometimes the nicest things happen to you when you least expect it.

Oops.

Like that. Hmmm . . . And that. Ahhhh . . .

Someday, she'd really have to send Brock a thank-you note . . .

ABOUT THE AUTHOR

Susan Johnson, award-winning author of nationally bestselling novels, lives in the country near North Branch, Minnesota. A former art historian, she considers the life of a writer the best of all possible worlds.

Researching her novels takes her to past and distant places, and bringing characters to life allows her imagination full rein, while the creative process offers occasional fascinating glimpses into the complicated machinery of the mind.

But perhaps most important . . . writing stories is fun.